War in the Land of Egypt

Emerging Voices
New International Fiction Series

The best way to learn about people and places far away

This series is designed to bring to North American readers the once-unheard voices of writers who have achieved wide acclaim at home, but were not recognized beyond the borders of their native lands. It publishes the best of the world's contemporary literature in translation.

Already published in the series

For a complete catalog please write to:
Interlink Publishing
46 Crosby Street, Northampton, MA 01060
Tel: (413) 582-7054 Fax: (413) 582-7057 e-mail: interpg@aol.com

War in the Land of Egypt

YUSUF AL-QA'ID

A PROTA BOOK
Translated by Olive and Lorne Kenney
and Christopher Tingley

INTERLINK BOOKS
An imprint of Interlink Publishing Group, Inc.
NEW YORK

First American edition published in 1998 by

INTERLINK BOOKS
An imprint of Interlink Publishing Group, Inc.
99 Seventh Avenue
Brooklyn, New York 11215

Originally published in Arabic as *Al-Harb fi Barr Misr* by Dar Ibn Rushd,
Beirut, 1978

The English translation was made under the auspices of PROTA (Project of
Translation from Arabic), Director: Salma Khadra Jayyusi, Cambridge,
Massachusetts and London.

Cover painting by Kamal Amin Awad, courtesy of The Royal Society of Fine Art,
Jordan National Gallery of Fine Art, Amman, Jordan.

Library of Congress Cataloging-in-Publication Data

Qa'id, Muhammad Yusuf.
   [Harb fi barr Misr. English]
   War in the land of Egypt / cYusuf al-Qa'id ; translated by Olive and
Lorne Kenny, and Christopher Tingley. — 1st American ed.
     p. cm.
   Originally published in Arabic: al-Harb fi barr Misr. Beirut :
Dar Ibn Rushd, 1978.
   ISBN 1-56656-227-9 (pbk.)
   I. Kenny, Olive E. II. Kenny, Lorne. III. Tingley, Christopher. IV. Title.
PJ7858.U3H3713 1998
892'.736—dc21
                                       97-21922
                                          CIP

Printed and bound in Canada
10 9 8 7 6 5 4 3 2 1

1
The *Umda**

I'm really not sure where to begin. I'd supposed that last night was historic in the life of our family, and I went to bed intoxicated with this feeling, but what's happened now has left me strangely puzzled. Which is historic, yesterday or today? I don't know.

Yesterday was a great day, the first time in many years that I'd known the meaning of happiness. The land they'd seized in 1954 was given back, and we found our dignity again. It's difficult to describe what yesterday was like. I wanted to die there and then, because nothing in the whole world could be greater than the joy I felt at our land being restored. The moment I heard of the court's just verdict,[†] I turned to face the south, sure that the red brick they'd placed under my father's head had now crumbled to dust. Before he died, he told me he'd find no rest as long as our land was in the hands of strangers, that the brick would remain hard and un-broken, denying him the peace of eternal sleep. It

---

* *Umda*: the chief of the district or village.

† The allusion here is to a law passed by the Sadat regime which decreed the restoration (within certain limits) of property nationalized under Nasser. The people to whom the land was returned were usually big landowners.

5

wouldn't crumble away, he said, till the time of true joy had come.

Now all the land had been returned. The sounds of joy rang out long after midnight—the ululations of the women and the rifle-shots of the men. As the night wore on I felt tired from a surfeit of happiness, and my ribs ached where my heart beat against them. When at last it was time to go to bed, I ordered the household not to wake me in the morning; I wanted to be left in peace to sleep as long as I liked, for the first time in more than twenty years. I had no work the following day, so why not enjoy all the glorious, restful idleness the old life used to offer us?

All this happened only yesterday; it's strange how fast time passes. At dawn this morning, before the cocks had started crowing in the yard, I was seized with a fit of coughing that wouldn't stop until I threw up; then I couldn't get back to sleep again.

It's been my habit of late to spend the night in my youngest wife's room. Some might say it's because she's 'new', and everything new has a special flavour, but that's not true, because my youngest wife isn't really new at all; in fact, she's been with me for quite a few years now. The real reason I make a point of spending the night in her room is that I feel comfortable with her. Hers is my favourite room.

After the cough I got a headache that hammered on the side and top of my head. It didn't look as if I'd get back to sleep now, so I got up and opened the window; the cool air would help my cough and headache. The sky was calm, the dawn air silent. Two stars were still out—forgotten by the night. Over the river I saw a comet in the sky; beside it were what looked like two flagstaffs embracing. There was a blue light in the air, mingled with the grey of the lonely daybreak hour.

I had nothing to do till sunrise and it was time for me to go into the *dawar*.* I called the maid and told her to bring some water so I could wash my face and perform the ritual ablutions before the morning prayer. She brought me a jug and a brass bowl. As she poured the water over my hands, a small bit of earth fell out of the jug and into my palm, but I didn't scold her or cry out, I didn't say a word. My wife brought me some tea, and I took the gold-rimmed glass and drew it to my mouth. The rim touched my lips and the tea ran freely over my tongue—then quickly I put the glass back on the low table. The tea was bitter; my wife had forgotten to put sugar in it! 'God protect us from evil,' I said to myself. I was afraid, because yesterday's happiness had made me feel on top of the world. At last I'd got even with those filthy swine! The land had been given back, and soon everything we'd lost would be returned to us. But I'm always nervous, even when life's good to me and I seem to have everything I want.

During the dawn prayer I almost made a slip in reciting the *fatiha*, the opening verses of the Koran, and the same thing happened with the blessings—I found it hard to concentrate. Then my left eyelid started twitching, and I knew for sure that something was up. When I'd finished my prayers, I asked my wife what day it was, and discovered it wasn't a Friday; this calmed me down a bit, because everyone knows that Friday brings its hour of bad luck.

My wife brought the breakfast tray, and as I lifted

---

* *Dawar*: the Umda's administrative centre for the village. It would probably be attached to his house but separate from it, having just one connecting door.

the cloth a cloud of steam rose from the fried eggs and glass of hot milk. I looked at each item in turn—eggs, broad beans, cheese and watercress—but my appetite had gone. I picked up the first loaf and broke it in half, then tore off a small piece and dipped it into something. I managed to force it down, but it was all I could eat. I washed my hands and drank a few glasses of tea, then said to my wife, 'Thanks be to God.'

Her eyelashes fluttered strangely, and her expression changed. 'Is something wrong with the food?' she asked.

'No,' I replied.

I told her I'd lost my appetite because I hadn't slept well after the happiness of the day before, but she wasn't convinced. She said she'd been worried about me since the early hours of the morning. I got up and went to get my outdoor clothes down from the wardrobe. She came close up behind me, her full breasts touching my back, but this only annoyed me. The more she pressed her firm bosom against my back, the more irritated I got. She pressed so close that I could feel the outline of her breasts. Remembering my plight, I said nothing. She held out her hand and asked if I was going to leave the house without breakfast, but my mind wasn't focused and I didn't answer. I left the apartment I'd built for her, opened the door to the old house and went in. All the rooms were shut and the smell of sleep pervaded the living-room. I went past my first wife's room—she's the mother of my grown children, and everyone calls her 'the old lady'. On the other side there's my second wife's room, then the children's rooms. I made my way to the cowshed, where the cattle were half asleep, their eyes closed, jaws moving slowly and lazily as they chewed over the previous night's food. Their troughs were empty, the bottoms looked almost polished where they had been licked clean. The dog was awake, though, and he wagged his tail and rubbed against my leg in a sign of recognition. I finished looking at the cattle and went in to the storerooms, where we keep farm produce, fertilizer, pesticides and tools. Everything was all right, so I went into the dawar. It was early, but no one seemed surprised at my unaccustomed energy. Some said it was because we'd got our land back; it wasn't just the land I had got back, they said, but life itself.

I sat down and started chain smoking. The nightwatchmen turned in their arms and ammunition belts, and after the hand-over the watchman on duty came up to me hesitantly, apparently afraid of something. When he handed me the ledger containing the night's messages, I told him angrily to read them out as he always did. His hand shook and he stammered out a few words. I snatched the messages from him, and immediately understood why he'd been scared: my youngest son had been called up for military service.

Now I saw it all. A day can be either white as milk or black as oven smoke, and this was a black one. Leaning back, I loudly invoked God's mercy on my father's soul. He was always suspicious of good things, and I'll never forget his words: 'If you find life bestowing a great blessing on you with its right hand, then its left is sure to be empty. You know why? Because what it gives with its right hand it takes back with its left.' I realized now that my father knew a lot of things I didn't.

The watchman was still standing in front of me, the message was still in my hand, and I freely admit that I had no idea how to react. I thought back long-ingly to the old days, when my father was always able to do the impossible—and so was I, in my younger days. I felt another headache coming on, and my thoughts raced like waves, carrying me off to distant horizons, and casting me back to a bench in the courtyard. I sent the watchman away, but the message was still there and the world seemed to close in on me. When my father found himself in a situation like this, he would laugh, and his eyes would sparkle green as the fields in spring. He'd smile and say that a great man could find any number of ways round his problems. As things stood, I couldn't see a single one.

The clerk from the telephone room arrived, sur-prised to see me up and about so early, and with despair written all over my face as I sat there wreathed in clouds of smoke. He looked at me closely, then called on God's help and asked what was wrong, but I didn't feel like answering. Several people told him what had happened, pointing to the bit of paper in my hand. I looked at him and he laughed, which made me angry; then he said it was simple enough and not worth getting so upset about. Coming close to me, he uttered just two words: 'The broker'.

I didn't understand what he meant, so he explained that this man could find a way around any problem, however difficult. Then I remembered him—the man everyone in the district called 'the broker'; nobody knew his real name any more. He'd fix any-thing, he could do anything you asked. He was originally a primary school teacher, but had been arrested for bribery or forgery, I can't remember which. His case was to have come up before the Lower Town Court, but there's so much red tape that it takes the courts a year to do what could be done in a day. So the case remained pending for years, first in the Lower Court, then in the District Court and finally in the High Court in Cairo, where he was finally found guilty. He appealed, but the appeal was rejected and his conviction upheld. He lost his teaching job but continued to act as a broker.

But I'm wandering off the point—it's strange how when you start telling a story the words spill out like an imam's prayer beads; each bead pulls the one behind it, so it's hard to stop anywhere or go back and clear up a point. As the clerk went on about the broker and how my problem could be solved, I hesitated. On the one hand I wanted my son to go into the army and learn some discipline. How much longer was he going to be pampered? I wouldn't be around to look after him for his whole life; one day he'd have to fend for himself. Yet on the other hand I couldn't bear to think of being parted from him, even for a day. He was my youngest child, and after being blessed with him I'd fallen ill. I went from town to town in search of a cure, but none of the doctors who examined me, or their medicine, was of any use. My condition got worse. I realized that ill health is the worst affliction anyone can be asked to bear, and that health is worth all the money in the world. In the end they removed my prostate—it was the only possible treatment, the doctors said; they had tried everything else. There was a form giving my consent to the operation. As I signed my name at the bottom, I told myself that no one must ever know; it must be a secret, buried in a deep and covered well. Loss of the prostate meant loss of my manhood, and if the people in the village got wind of it they might say I was no longer fit to be their umda, because the umda has to be a complete man. I tried to make things easier by telling myself I had any number of children, but when I got back I felt depressed and my love for my youngest son grew stronger. People said I loved him so much because his mother was my newest wife, a girl the same age as my own children, but no one knew the real reason.

When I got back from hospital, I couldn't decide which of my three wives to live with. I pondered my recent relations with them. My first wife couldn't stand the sight of me, and my second was mortified because I'd married again, so that left the third. I consoled myself by saying it was better for only one of them to be let into the secret than all three.

From that moment on, my life changed. I slept less and would wake up several times a night; now that I was denied the blessing of sleep, the night seemed like a bad dream. I moved the radio next to my bed, and got angry when the programmes stopped with more than half the night still to go—which I had to spend alone. I thought longingly of days gone by, when the nights were never long enough for sleep, and as time went on I grew more and more afraid of my youngest wife, with her youth and freshness. But there was no excuse for staying away from her. I could hardly leave her alone in such a big apartment, so I prayed for God's help and spent the torture they call night in her room, repeatedly asking myself why we have to suffer like this and why a person can't just die suddenly, instead of having to endure this slow death.

But let me get back to the business about my son. As I said before, I couldn't bear to be parted from him even for a moment, but there was another very good reason to keep him with me: none of his brothers had ever done their military service. My eldest son was exempt under the law covering the sons of umdas, and the next because, having memorized the Holy Koran, he carried God's word in his bosom and was regarded as a *faqih*.* As for the third, I paid a cool twenty Egyptian pounds for him not be called up, and a pound was really worth something in those days—as much as twenty pounds in these miserable times. As for my fourth son, his mother was the most beautiful woman in the village . . . Ah, the good times have gone now, and a lot of things with them! Will they ever return? Yes, I believe they will—especially when you consider the recent good omens. I divorced the mother of this fourth son—a secret divorce, just on paper—so officially he became her sole means of support.

Before we go any further, let me make it perfectly clear that I'm not ashamed to admit all this. In fact, let's talk about it here and now, so you can appreciate just how I feel. I realize you might be angry. 'Does this Egyptian have no sense of shame or dishonour,' you may wonder, 'fiddling things so his sons don't do their bit to defend their country? No matter what changes are made to the call-up laws, he always finds some clever way of making sure they avoid military service! Aren't we all Egypt's sons?' You may go on, 'It's our country, and it's our duty to defend it body and soul.' Besides, as umda, it's my responsibility to see that everyone does his military service. So how come I arranged for my own children to escape the call-up? What would the villagers say if they knew all this? I can imagine how you must feel, and I realize the inevitable conclusion your questions might lead

---

* *Faqih* : in popular usage, a reciter of the Koran.

you to: that I arranged for my sons to evade their military service at a time when Egypt was fighting three vital wars that affected its whole destiny. Faced with all these questions, I despair of getting you to understand my position. I don't know if you can understand the situation I was in.

First, let me say that I'm a patriot and I love the land of Egypt; the deep love of the Nile Valley runs in my blood. I inherited that feeling from my father, as he did from his father and his grandfather before him. It's a love with roots in history, more real than all the talk of today's generation, whose love for Egypt is mere words. My great-grandfather was one of the unknown soldiers who defended Egypt's honour alongside Ahmad Pasha Urabi,* and there's no better evidence of true patriotism than that. Yet I never even mention the martyrdom of a member of our family in Urabi's uprising. It's my own private secret, and this is the first time I've ever spoken about it.

You know, of course, that I'm now an umda. My father used to say that if any of us had gone into the armed forces, the family tree would have been shaken, would have been bent and bowed almost to the ground, and the family could never have traced its origins back to the times of the Mamelukes and Turks in Egypt; so you'll appreciate that I've no right to take stupid risks with it. Personally I would have been happy to see my children go into the army; in fact it's an honour to serve in the armed forces. The whole thing followed from my original mistake of

---

* Ahmad Pasha Urabi: an Egyptian colonel of peasant origin who in 1882 led a revolt against Anglo-French control of Egypt and the influential Mamelukes, a soldier class of Turkish or Circassian origin.

having my eldest son exempted. After that, each son would compare himself with his elder brother, and when I tried to argue the point, they had an answer as sharp as a sword: 'None of the others has done military service!'

'The world's changed,' I'd answer, 'and we must change with it.'

I would have liked my youngest son to go into the armed forces. But suppose his mother compared herself with the two senior wives and demanded the same treatment for her son? What if she looked me straight in the eye and said, 'Isn't it enough that I have to put up with your impotence?' She was the only one who knew my secret; she was the most trustworthy of my three wives, and hers was the only bed I'd slept in since I came back from hospital. But the secret might have come out if her son was called up, and the whole village might have found out. How can we imagine the feelings of a mother whose only son gets sent into the firing-line? Military life's not what it used to be in the old days; now the army fights real wars, with fighting and shelling, and God only knows when it will end. So I had to do something, there was just no choice—who would send his own son to be killed? So I would have to see the broker.

There was another thing too: for years my youngest wife wanted a brother for her son. I don't know why she never got pregnant again; in the country these things are women's secrets, and men don't talk about them. But when I told her about my operation she cried and said she wished she'd known before, so she could have saved her son from the bitterness of spending his whole life as an only child. I tried to console her, saying that he'd got a whole army of brothers, but she said they were only half-brothers. So now I was caught up in all this mess; but one thing I did know—whatever happened, my youngest son wasn't going very far from me!

I made my decision—I'd go and see the broker. I relaxed, feeling my troubles would soon be over. I'd give the broker whatever he asked, and use my connections, friends, relations, and above all my money, to back his efforts up. Everybody knows what the motto is these days: 'If you've got a piastre, you're worth a piastre.' Well, I have millions of piastres, thank God, and as long as the piastre is still the god everyone lives by, I have nothing to fear. It won't be long before they start operating on people in this country, taking out their hearts and sticking gold pounds in their place, so they pump out gold piastres instead of red and white blood cells. When this time comes we'll get our prestige and reputation back, and we'll be kings of Egypt again.

I had a rest, then got up and went into the house, where my youngest son was still asleep. My blood boiled as I looked at him—sleeping till the noon call to prayer! 'My God,' I said to myself, 'there's only one way to smarten him up, and that's to send him to the front! But what can you do with things the way they are?' I told my wife to get my travelling clothes ready. In the village I wear a *gallabiyya* like everyone else—although mine are made of an imported material that's almost impossible to find in the province. But when I travel (when I leave the village, that is), I wear a suit and dark glasses, sprinkle on cologne, and look sharper than any fine gentleman, however high his position and salary.

I told my wife I was going to the district town. No one in the house ever asks about my movements except my youngest wife, this being a privilege I've granted her. She didn't ask why I was going. I thought of telling her, so I would seem important, an influential man who could do the impossible, but I was afraid the story would get passed on from one mouth to the next, with details and explanations added along the way. My father taught me that it's difficult to bring something off if more than two people know about it. We're the upper class, sons of good families, and everyone's jealous of us—that's why I have to be discreet. But one day my wife would find out about everything I'd done, and then she'd think me bigger than a mountain, stronger than a lion.

I ordered a car and waited for it outside the house. I climbed into the back seat. The clerk from the telephone room, who was coming with me, shut the door behind me and got in next to the driver. He saw my frowning face in the mirror and smiled back at me. He kept trying to cheer me up, saying that it was a simple matter, but I didn't deign to reply. I can't say I was happy during our journey, but neither was I sad. A lot of people from the village saw me and signalled to the car to stop so they could greet me. One of them said he supposed I must be going to Cairo to thank high-ranking people in the government because my land had been restored. I said nothing—I didn't confirm what he said or deny it. I thought that was the best thing to do—it would stop people trying to find out the real reason for my journey. On the way the car passed some of the land that had been returned, and this reminded me of all the events of the previous day. My thoughts went back to my father. Before he died, he said to me, 'Our rights are bound to be restored one day.' 'God alone knows what the future holds,' I replied. It had been a painful business, but now that those days have gone for ever, I don't mind telling you about it by way of digression.

About two years after Nasser's military coup my father divided up his land among my brothers, my sisters and myself. There was one piece of land that we'd bought recently, but the lengthy special registration procedures hadn't been completed, so it wasn't shared out with the rest.

One morning some committees sent by the military junta arrived with an officer who said he represented headquarters. They said they had documents showing that our father was of Turkish origin, and that the steps he'd taken to acquire Egyptian nationality weren't legally valid. So they were going to confiscate the piece of land which was then being registered in his name. Since our mother and both her parents were Egyptian and we'd all been born in Egypt, they wouldn't take all our land, but would just apply the Agrarian Reform Law and take whatever we owned above the prescribed limits. They didn't seize my sisters' lands, and the law didn't apply to my younger brothers, but my case was different. There was a lot of land registered in my name, because my father had favoured me with more than my brothers. In addition, my first wife had owned some land which she put in my name after we were married, and this had officially become my property too. They seized all my extra land, and I ended up with a mere two hundred *feddans*.

When they took away our title to the land, it was more than my father could bear, and that day he had a stroke. His right side was paralysed, and he couldn't move his right hand, his right foot or the right side of his mouth. It was a terrible time. People who had full stomachs only in their dreams now dared to defy us, whereas just a few days before no villager would have dared pass my father without getting off his donkey. Gone were the days when I'd seen my father take anyone who disobeyed his orders and tie him to the eucalyptus tree that still stands in our courtyard. Time is a cruel destroyer.

The day after the military seized our land, the hired hands and regular labourers and supervisors started acting differently towards us. People said openly, with vengeful satisfaction, that they were glad my father was ill—sometimes they even said it in front of me. The future looked bleak. I was afraid of dying before the land was returned to me, because that would mean, quite simply, dying while having lost faith in many principles, most of all the belief that Good ultimately triumphs in this world. But it seems that God, may He be praised, did not wish me to meet Him with my spirit impaired in this way. Unexpectedly and suddenly, dawn broke.

The government no longer controlled our property, and part of our land was returned to us. Then I filed a legal suit to prove that the blood that flowed in my father's veins was Egyptian, that blue blood had never flowed in our veins, and that the founder of our line had overseen the building of the Great Pyramid of Cheops. This had been established, historically and scientifically, in excavations in one of our fields at the beginning of the year. Then yesterday came the judgement returning our land. I was amazed at how fast it had been issued, for justice is a notoriously slow business in Egypt, but it seems there were instructions to speed up the process of restoring rights to victims of injustice like us. When I heard the news, I said, 'The important thing isn't what's been returned so far, but what will be returned in the days ahead.'

My energy returned, my old spirit broke out from under the rubble of injustice, and once again I experienced the joy of days gone by. I decided to stand for the next parliamentary elections. We had to sweep away that bunch of kids called the Committee of the Arab Socialist Union once and for all! Even if they offered to make me secretary-general I would refuse; it's them or me. Let them be content with the last sixteen years, when they ran things the way they wanted, with all their clapping and speechmaking! The sons of good families are going to have a say in things again, and who knows, one of my sons might be given a top position. My father used to say that there are two kinds of people in the land of Egypt: sons of good families and sons of dogs. In the countryside, sons of good families are the people who own more than a hundred feddans; the ones who don't own any land are the second kind. Between the two extremes is a long ladder, with all kinds of people standing on it—small landowners, regular labourers, hired hands and the unemployed. I'm telling you all this to make you understand how happy I was last night—then you'll believe me when I say I didn't sleep a wink.

The way things are now, my son won't be called up. If you lived in Egypt in the early fifties, you'll understand what I'm saying; you'll see the force of it and find a thousand reasons for excusing me. On the other hand, if you're one of those people who've drunk in the language of these strange times with their mother's milk, then you won't even try to understand or make allowances. But I pin my hopes on the days to come—they'll make this whole business clear to you. Our generation's unlucky. It wasn't just our land, prestige and authority that the army coup took away; sixteen years just dropped out of our lives, and we could have done a lot in those years for the Egypt we love so much. But through God's mercy we're safe again now, the nightmare's over; hatred has gone and love remains. When will this senseless war end? Peace is a thousand times better than shelling and killing.

When we reached the town of Itai al-Baroud, the clerk directed the driver to the broker's house; when we arrived, he got out to see if the man was at home, while I stayed in the car. In the morning the clerk had said I shouldn't go in person. He even offered to bring the broker to see me in the village, but I said no, because the visit would have aroused people's curiosity. Everyone knows the broker comes for illegal purposes, and besides, if he turned up at such a happy moment, when our land had just been returned, our enemies would be suspicious about the verdict, would think there might have been bribery and 'special contacts'; and—who knows?—this might cause problems for me and my children in the future.

The clerk returned and loudly asked me to go in. He added the word 'Bey' to my name, a title from the good old days which I'd long since forgotten. I got out, made my way slowly into the broker's living-room, and sat down to wait for him.

The clerk explained that the broker was asleep—I must say, I envied him his peace of mind. When he appeared he smelled of daytime sleep, and his eyes were swollen. From the red creases on his right cheek it was clear he'd been sleeping on a straw mat without a pillow, or else his head had rolled off the pillow when he'd moved in his sleep, and he'd just slept on like that without waking up. Sitting opposite, he welcomed me and asked how everything was. He could see from my face, he said, that I was worried about something, so I told him what had happened.

He lit a cigarette and offered me one, but I preferred not to change my usual brand of imported cigarettes. Then he asked if I'd ever arranged for my son's call-up to be postponed before. Surely my children went to school, he said, and this son of mine must be studying now, so he had the right to put off his military service till he's reached the maximum number of postponements. I laughed to hide my sadness and anger, then told him that unfortunately the boy was a hopeless failure and didn't even have his preparatory school certificates. I'd given him every facility to help him pass, and still he failed year after year. I paid for him to enrol again, and when he failed again, I sent him to a private school in the district town. But after I'd paid the fees his mother refused to let him go, because she was afraid of what his half-brothers might do to him. She'd had a dream, she said, in which they poisoned him because they were jealous, and she couldn't bear to be parted from him. If I insisted on his being educated, she said, then she'd go with him to the town. I refused to let her go. Then, a few days later, she came out with the strangest demand imaginable. She insisted that he leave school altogether, because he was sure to fail, and that would lead to psychological traumas that might affect him for the rest of his life! In any case, she said, suppose he got a university degree, what use would that be to him? Work was for people who didn't have enough to eat at home.

22

The broker had lit a second cigarette, and as he listened he blew smoke-rings and watched them drift about the room. Then he spoke. Although it would be very much to his advantage, he said, for my son not be called up, a sense of duty compelled him to advise me that the only way to make a man of my son was to let him go into the army; in fact, if he didn't do his military service, my last chance in that direction would be lost. I told him I appreciated his advice and was grateful for it, but added that people often have private reasons for doing things and that I was in a difficult and complicated situation. I had to keep the boy with me; if his summons had come at some other time, I would have thrown him straight into the firing-line. The broker clearly wasn't convinced. Then he got down to brass tacks, criticizing me for not coming to see him right at the beginning. I showed my surprise. Surely this was the beginning, I said. I hadn't been to see anyone else. No, he said. By 'beginning' he meant my son's childhood. I should have come to see him as soon as the boy was born and told him I didn't want the boy to serve in the army. Then he would have dealt with the situation, and things would have been worked out with no trouble. It wouldn't have cost me one *millim*.

As he spoke, he lost his drowsy, lazy, unenthusiastic air. 'Do you know', he asked, 'why your son was called up today? Because a few months ago he went to the district town to get an identity card. One of the forms that has to be filled in to get this card is sent to the recruiting office in Cairo, so they can check whether someone's done his military service or not, and if he hasn't then he's immediately issued call-up papers. If I'd known, I would have arranged things with the clerk of the Civil Registry Office, because there's a simple, standard way out at this stage: the call-up papers wouldn't have been sent to Cairo, and no one would ever have known anything about your son. It's because he acted without consulting you— which means I didn't know anything about it either —that we have a problem now. Well, we have to find a way out. It won't be easy, but it's not hopeless either, it's not impossible. I'll deal with it.'

I felt my face relax and began to calm down. We all make mistakes, I told him, and he was the one person who could put things right. We created a lot of problems, I said, because we had such complete confidence in his ability to solve them.

He was at my service, he assured me. Then he took my son's papers and asked us to come back in a couple of days. The clerk reminded him about the call-up papers, but the broker said he'd be able to get a deferment for a few days. He promised to contact the man in charge of conscription and ask him to ignore the papers for a week or so until he, the broker, had found some solution to the problem. His yellowing teeth gleamed as he implied, with a smile, that the official in charge of conscription co-operated with him over many matters.

As we walked away from the house, I felt a gnawing sense of unease. I was worried about the broker's lack of enthusiasm, since everyone who'd dealt with him before always said he was so reassuring. Maybe it was because I'm an umda and, as such, the official embodiment of the government itself; or maybe he was apprehensive because the clerk heard everything and could be used as a witness against him. I decided to send the clerk back in to reassure him, to explain that it's a habit of mine never to take any trip on my own but always to have a watchman or a clerk with me.

Back home, no one knew anything about what had happened. I went out to the dawar and warned the clerk and the watchman on duty not to say anything to anyone about the call-up papers. The clerk laughed and said that as far as he was concerned the papers had never arrived; it hadn't been recorded in the books or official records.

Then I dealt with some outstanding problems. The estate clerk brought me details of the land which, thanks to the just verdict of the court, was due to be restored; I was to prepare to take it over. Attached to the report was a list of the peasants who'd been farming the land since its seizure: some of them had tenancy agreements, others were buying the land in easy instalments for ridiculously low sums. I looked over the papers. Tomorrow I'll send the clerk to the court to find out when the copy of the decision will be ready, so the execution order can be issued. In the meantime I'll have to judge the mood of the people. I don't know whether they'll give up the land peacefully, with no hard feelings, or whether I'll have to call in the police, who, thank God, are there to restore the rights of downtrodden people like us. I will refuse to take over any land with tenants still on it; I'd rather not have it back at all than have it on those terms. The rent from one feddan is only thirty pounds a year, and then there are various taxes, as well as fees and deferred debts, whereas if I take over a feddan of land directly, making it part of my own great estate and cultivating it myself, I'll make five hundred pounds a year net. What's more, if I agreed to take the land with tenants on it, I wouldn't be able to evict them. I'd better get things straight now, I thought—although, as a matter of fact, I'm confident the laws dealing with the relationship between landlord and tenant are going to be changed. Who would have believed the land would be given back to us? And now that the impossible has happened, a lot of abuses are going to be put right, and we'll soon be back to the old ways. As our forefathers said, 'The man who's blessed with patience will achieve his heart's desire.'

Night fell. I always had supper in the dawar when there were guests, but tonight there weren't any and I decided to eat at home, in the apartment of my youngest wife—she'd remain my youngest wife, since I wouldn't marry again now. 'The old lady' was standing at the door of her room as I passed, and she muttered something when she saw me. Remembering the business of my son, I told myself that she and her children would be the first to gloat if it ever came out. I had something to eat and washed it down with tea, giving thanks to God. Then I sat down at my wife's side and told her what had happened, assuring her she wouldn't be separated from her son. But as I talked, I realized that she was young and inexperienced; she couldn't really take in the meaning of what had happened. I felt I'd been unfair to her, because she doesn't know much about the world of men.

Next morning the clerk went to see the broker, and his words were full of reassurance when he returned —although he said that, judging by the conversation, the broker would pitch things high when it came to fixing a price for his services. I went to see the broker again at the time we'd arranged, and met with the same reception as before—the man seems to have an unenthusiastic attitude to life. There were two possible solutions, he said. The first was easy, foolproof and safe, the second difficult and complicated. The

easy solution, which wouldn't cost very much, involved taking out papers for my son to go abroad; he
should then stay there until the whole call-up business had died down. I rejected this solution out of
hand. How could he go abroad? There was no question whatever of my son leaving me. 'That solution's
out then,' he said, and moved on to the second, running through a complex procedure which I didn't
understand at first. When I finally got it, I felt nervous: it was obvious that all kinds of people would
have to be involved. But what could I do? When you
need something you don't have much choice. I
thought of putting off the agreement till the following day, so I could think it over calmly on my own,
but the clerk pleaded with me, saying it wasn't worth
getting worked up about, that we'd almost got things
sorted out. So I told the broker I'd agree to his plan,
but then stopped and thought over the last part of it,
according to which my son was to live well away
from the village till the whole thing was over. Laughing, I said my son could perhaps leave the village for
a fortnight or even a month, but the broker looked at
me and said, slowly and quietly, that my son's absence from the village would be a long one, perhaps
as much as five years. There was no alternative if the
arrangement was to remain secret. My son's presence
in the village would be clear-cut evidence that would
land us all in prison. I said I'd wanted to give him
one last chance to get his preparatory school certificate from a private school somewhere.

'What are you talking about?' cried the broker.
'Your son's supposed to be in the army. No schools
and no education!' Then he laughed and said that
preparatory or secondary school certificates weren't
really a problem. You could buy them in Cairo, he

said, and he personally knew a doctor in the Abbasiya district who had a whole stock of them. Each certificate was priced according to the type, the year, the subject and the final grade. I felt incredibly uneasy. I'm making a terrible mistake, I thought, protecting my son from the army only to land him in a situation with no future.

I went back to his mother and told her what had happened, suggesting she go back to her home village. I was surprised when she refused, but it seemed she was afraid for herself and her son—she comes from a big family with many branches; they have a lot of enemies and are involved in a lot of feuds. I couldn't believe my ears when she said she wanted to rent an apartment in the district town and live there with her son. I could visit her three times a week, she said, or else buy a car, live in town with her and drive in to the village every day. I thought she must be joking, because she knows I can't live any distance from the village. I'm like a fish and the village is the great open sea—I'd die if I had to live outside it for a minute. The only life I have is here. In any case, how could I leave the village with the good days almost here and the signs of a happy future appearing for the first time? I suspected her motives. Here in the village I could keep an eye on her and no one could creep into her room, but how did I know what would happen if she moved into town with her feckless son? I thought it over for a long time. If I'd known it would come to this, I thought, I would have let my son be sent to the army.

I went to my bedroom and tried to sleep, but couldn't. As I tossed and turned, the bed creaked under me, reminding me of the days when I was a real man. Then I considered one aspect of the problem which hadn't occurred to me before: the broker asked me to find a young man the same age as my son, born on exactly the same day, and with similar features, so he could be taken in my son's place. When we got back, the clerk had started going through the village register of births and deaths. Finally he handed me a small piece of paper with the name 'Masri'* written on it. Angrily, I told him to find someone else. You'd laugh if I told you why—you probably wouldn't believe me.

The fact is, this boy Masri is the son of a retired watchman, and is known throughout the village for his intelligence and his good record at school; he is always top of his class, and I'd made no secret of my admiration for him. How often had I felt jealous and wished he was my own son! I clenched my fists in frustration at the unfathomable way life deals with people, how it gives the earring to the person with no ear, as we Egyptians say. Masri left school the previous year because he had no brothers, only sisters, and his father couldn't afford to let him continue his studies in the town when he needs someone to look after the three feddans of land he leased under the Agrarian Reform. I sat and thought about life's vagaries. My son, who I could educate in China if I wanted, is a failure, while this young man, who couldn't even afford a change of clothes, is brilliant and successful. As the only boy of six children, he was exempt from military service, whereas my own son, who has not completed his education, has to be called up.

The clerk came back and insisted that Masri was the most suitable person. I begged him to find some-

---

* Masri: the word means 'Egyptian' in Arabic.

one else, because I'm not inhuman; I do have a heart, and I don't like to be unjust to anyone. If it was simply a question of finding another young man, the clerk said, there were plenty besides Masri, and he handed me a list of male children born on the same day as my son. I looked over the names and families, but he was right: the only suitable one was Masri.

The clerk asked why I was hesitating—after all, in a way I was doing Masri a favour. The land they were farming was going to be taken back and given to me, and the family's sole source of income would be his father's wages, which were less than six pounds a month. Masri would have to look for work, and if he didn't find any he'd volunteer for the army anyway; so by sending Masri to the army in my son's place I'd be giving him a good chance to earn his living and help support his family. All his needs would be taken care of, he'd have food, drink, clothing and a roof over his head, and I'd be responsible for looking after his people here. Could they ever have dreamed of anything like that?

The clerk was reassuring. Serving in the army, he said, was the only way to get a guaranteed job, because there's a regulation that a person has to be given a secure government job as soon as his period of service is up. And if he doesn't want to leave the forces, he can sign up again and rise to a high rank with a good salary. Either way, when you thought about it, what was going to happen to Masri was greatly to his advantage.

The clerk swore that Masri had been looking for an army enlistment form anyway. He'd been to the post office the day before to ask about it, and they'd told him that the form's given out by the deputy recruiting officer at the head office. The real reason for all this was that Masri's family had heard the news about the land taken under the Agrarian Reform being restored to its rightful owners, and the world had seemed to close in on them. They'd also heard about a peasant in a neighbouring village who'd refused to give up his land and had been killed by the police. Masri was going into the army anyway, either in his own name or as a replacement for somebody else, and it didn't matter whether he volunteered or went as the umda's son.

Far from convinced, I floundered as I tried to work out the rights and wrongs of the case. My trouble is that my conscience always pricks me, calling me to account for every little thing I do. That's what you have to put up with if you're the son of a good family, who's had decent people to bring him up properly and spend money on his schooling—not like these people without any education. The clerk kept on talking, trying to convince me that what I was doing was chiefly in the interests of the watchman and his son, and only incidentally in the interests of my own son. When the clerk was tired of talking and I was tired of listening, I finally agreed.

'Then,' said the clerk, as he left for home, 'we'll go ahead with God's blessing.'

2
The Broker

The only pleasure I get these days is sleep. Wake up so you can go back to sleep again—that's my philosophy, and I act on it every day. I just go on tossing and turning from side to side, right to left, first on my face, then onto my back, like an irrigation screw wearing itself out in an unending dizzy spin. Only when my body protests at all the sleep do I finally wake up, my bones aching, eyes swollen, my mind seeming to float on a sea of calm.

When people pass my house knowing I'm asleep, do you know what they do? They call out, 'When the bloodsucker's asleep it's a blessing for the rest of us!' And yet I've never been unjust to anyone—in fact I've spent my whole life helping people. But it's always the same: the moment I've solved someone's problem and it's time to pay up, suddenly I'm a bloodsucker!

That day I was asleep as usual, dreaming the same old dream that helps lessen my life's misery. I dream that the director of education is apologizing to me at a public meeting, asking me to go back to my job as a teacher. I stipulate that in view of my seniority I should be made a headmaster forthwith, and the director-general agrees to all my conditions, apologizing again, in the name of the Ministry of Education. I accept his apology and say I'll go to school the next day.

At that moment I was roused from my slumber by the sound of a car horn. This annoyed me, because I wanted to go on living the dream a little longer. The car honked again. It was strange, because there aren't many cars in our town and my customers aren't the sort who own them. A man who travels by car knows all the top people and uses his family and friends to run his affairs. He's got as many avenues and as many schemes up his sleeve as he's got hairs on his head. It's the poor and wretched who come to see me, the people without too many chances in life—the sort who, as we say, always have the door shut in their faces.

One of my children came and told me we had visitors, strangers, and I went out to find the umda of one of the villages in our district. Well, well, I thought, what are things coming to? Umdas are just paper tigers these days; they'd blow away if you looked at them. Gone are the days when umdas could do the impossible.

I was still in my nightgown. My throat was dry, so I gulped down a little water before going into the reception-room where the umda was sitting. Then my heart sank, because I saw that this umda was one of the richest men in the district. That might seem a good omen, but in fact it's always the rich who haggle over the fee; the poor pay up without a word, though I don't know where they get the money. Still, I had no work on hand at the time. Business was bad, so I told myself one eye was better than being completely blind.

The umda wasn't alone in the reception-room.

There was a stranger with him, but when I got closer I recognized him as the clerk in charge of the telephone under the umda's jurisdiction. I shook hands and sat down, and we exchanged the usual polite talk about each other's health and how things were going, and what was happening in the world, and I mouthed the courtesies expected on such an occasion. In as friendly a voice as I could muster, I said that light had entered our house, that the Prophet was visiting us today, and how overjoyed I was by the honour his excellency the umda was bestowing on our humble abode. The clerk told me I should congratulate the umda, since an official order for the restoration of his land had been issued the day before. A big celebration had been held in the village, he said, to which every person of note in the district should have been invited, including myself, but the festivities had been arranged at such short notice that the umda had been unable to issue any invitations. Anyway, the main festivities had been postponed till the day the land was actually handed over, and I was invited, as of now, to attend the magnificent celebration.

I knew well enough that the clerk was lying; that it hadn't even entered their heads to invite me, and that our present meeting had forced him into saying it. Still, I pretended to believe him and congratulated the umda, saying that a victory for him was a victory for all of us—not realizing at the time just what that 'all of us' meant. As I rose to embrace the umda, I caught sight of my face in the big mirror opposite. It looked a happy face, and that made me think it must belong to someone else—no doubt there were other people living inside me! I didn't grasp the full significance of what the clerk had said about the business of the land and all the rest of it, but the joy I pretended to feel had forced me out of my lethargy, bringing a sense of inner peace that was quite intoxicating. This was surely a good omen! The umda had had his land taken from him, and its return was more important for his children than for him. But I'd lost my job, my dignity and my children's future. Since the day I could no longer tell the pupils to stand up or sit down in class, I'd been like a cripple or a barren palm-tree. The words of the umda's clerk filled me with fresh reassurance. If the umda's land had been restored, surely my dignity, position and standing would come back too. It was only a matter of time.

There was a silence after the congratulations because we couldn't find anything else to say to each other. Tea arrived, and I proceeded to serve it. The umda took a packet of cigarettes from his pocket, a brand I'd never seen before, and I jumped to fetch a packet from my bedroom. We offered each other cigarettes, each begging the other to accept with the weightiest of oaths. I mentioned the duties of a host and the rules governing hospitality, but the umda settled the matter by saying we belonged to the same family and so he was in his own house. After all, he said, there should be no distinctions between the members of one family.

With the tea and cigarettes, I felt my old longing for action return to me. Having decided to get straight to the point, I asked, 'How's everything going?'

'Fine, God willing,' answered the clerk.

The umda cleared his throat and spat into a perfumed handkerchief, then looked around, and I got up and shut both reception-room doors, the one leading back into the house and the one giving onto the street. When I came back I took a seat directly opposite the umda.

36

I listened to what he had to say, while the clerk, just to make his presence felt, put in the odd word to correct the information the umda was giving me or to explain something I didn't understand. The situation was clear enough, and it was going to be a hard nut to crack. I wondered if any of my standard methods would do it. His problem, to put it in a nutshell, was that he didn't want his son to do his military service. If he didn't want to go into further details, that was his privilege. People have their secrets, and even their own brothers often don't know what these are. In fact, all of us are just miserable bundles of secrets.

I had several standard solutions to hand. A man could, I said, divorce his wife so that the son becomes the sole support of his divorced mother. To my astonishment the umda violently opposed such a solution. In fact, his newest wife had borne him just the one son, which made her situation ideal, but the umda raised his hand and said, in a tone that brooked no argument, that it was quite out of the question.

I tried to argue, but he cut me off. I would have to come up with something else, he said, rather than wasting a lot of time and effort on a solution he would never accept.

I looked away. This man was an umda, and traditional solutions like cutting off one of the boy's fingers or pouring acid in his eyes wouldn't fool anyone. I was baffled. I didn't want to close all the doors. Couldn't I keep one open just a chink? I asked for time to think things over, but he was impatient for a solution and clearly wasn't going to budge till I'd found a way out. I said I'd have to consult some other people, and he replied that I wasn't to worry about the expense, because he had any amount of money. Rich people always go on like that to start with, but when it comes to paying up—you might as well expect the stars to come out at noon! I told him it wasn't easy and there'd be difficulties, but he said he was sure I was more than equal to a little problem like this.

As he was about to leave, he came right up to me, anxiously looked from side to side and then told me again how careful I had to be. Anything could happen these days, he said, and no matter how clever you are, something can always go wrong. It was a delicate game I'd be playing, and I could easily come unstuck.

He left me to think over what had happened to me in the past. I think the umda's already told you about that—how I was dismissed from my job as a teacher —and I'm grateful to him for sparing me the unpleasant task of going into it again. It's distressing, like a great weight on my heart. How can I put it? Nothing I do now gives me any pleasure or satisfaction. I used to be a primary school teacher like thousands of others in the land of Egypt, but now when my pupils meet me in the street they look the other way.

I honestly can't remember how it all began. I've got a sister whose husband died when she was very young, leaving her with a son. She became what we country people call a *hagala*, a widow, and she had no one in the world except me. Her husband had left her five feddans, but that only complicated her prospects of marrying again, because it made us suspect everyone who wanted to marry her of having his eye on the land. So she never remarried.

Time flies, and before we knew it her son had reached the age for military service. As the sole support of his widowed mother, he legally was entitled to exemption, and the officials in the district administration said we had to get the appropriate bit of paper from the recruiting office in Alexandria.

Laugh if you like, but I wish with all my heart we'd never gone to Alexandria that day; it was the unluckiest day of my life. I remember it well enough. It was December, and cold enough in the village to freeze your fingers, but in Alexandria it was a pleasant, warm day. I was on my way to demand a right that was as clear as the noonday sun when I fell into a trap called the Bottomless Government Pit—a trap open night and day. We met an officer from a village near mine. He had an eagle on his shoulder and said he was a former volunteer who'd risen through the ranks to become a major.

A peasant can smell another peasant from here to China, and when he heard me talking at the door he came and asked what village I was from. My accent and dialect, he said, reminded him of waterwheels and fields and threshing machines and irrigation screws. After we'd talked for a while we went to his house, where he assured me there was no problem and asked for five pounds. The money, he said, was to give to some people at the army camp—he'd divorce his wife if he kept a millim himself! I gave him what he asked for, we spent two nights at his house and then came back to the village with my sister's son. He had all the necessary papers.

The officer had told me to call at his house or his office if I ever needed anything for anyone in my village or the nearby villages and he'd help me out. He was elderly—obviously due for retirement in a few months—and I suppose this made him rash enough to take risks.

The people in the village soon heard the story: I'd

been to Alexandria with my nephew, they said, and we came right back with the exemption certificate in hand. This call-up business comes up in every household, and everyone's always looking for a way out. A lot of the villagers started coming to me, and I found myself taking the train to Alexandria every afternoon, till I got so busy I rented a flat there and married a second wife, a fair-skinned city woman born and raised in the days of prosperity.

Things were going very well, the officer working miracles every day. I knew, of course, that a lot of the problems were simple and that the officer hardly had to lift a finger to solve them, but that didn't stop him going on about how hard it was to make ends meet and how expensive everything was getting. It wasn't easy getting hold of people, he said. Eventually there was so much business that other people in the district administration were brought in on it.

People found out what I was doing. Complaints were sent to the authorities, and a warrant for my arrest was issued. They came for me in my flat in Alexandria and, to my shame, I had to flee to the village at dawn, still in my pyjamas.

An investigation began: questions, papers, inquiries; an officer was brought in, the bureau of investigation, detectives. I was arrested, then let out on bail but suspended from my job, and had no way of making a living. I asked for help from the people I'd done favours for before. It's true I'd made a lot of money, more and more as time went on, but I hadn't saved any. The Lord giveth, I'd told myself, and the Lord taketh away!

I hired a well-known lawyer, but my Alexandria wife testified against me; she said she was unhappy about what I'd been doing. I thought of divorcing her, but people told me that wouldn't help—she'd just drag me through the courts, and that would mean paying alimony and the rest of the dowry, on top of legal fees. I had enough problems as it was, so I just left her in the air, neither married nor divorced. I thought she'd pursue me wherever I went, but I heard nothing of her for several months, and when I finally made inquiries I found she'd married some other man while she was still married to me. That was wonderful news, because now I thought I might be able to get her put in prison, but when I went looking for her, I couldn't find her; the earth had just swallowed her up. After searching high and low, I discovered that the man she'd married worked in Libya and she'd gone to join him there.

I forgot to mention that this officer from my district was thrown out in a purge, and I was compulsorily retired. Still, they hadn't seized any papers to use against me, I hadn't confessed, and no prosecution witnesses had come forward except my wife—and she wasn't around any more. Everyone assured me I'd get off, but in court they said there was a political dimension to the case because national defence was involved: how could the younger generation, the future men of Egypt, be entrusted to a man who spent his afternoons helping people evade their duty to defend their country? 'The reason you've been retired', my lawyer said, 'is that the law's gone to pot, may God help Egypt! If the law had any teeth, you'd have got off scot-free.'

In those days I didn't realize that what I was doing had anything to do with politics, or with national defence against the enemies of the revolution. As far as I was concerned, I was just easing some of the burdens of the poor and wretched who couldn't tell the letter 'a' from a corncob. Three-quarters of the people in our village are illiterate, and I was making up for their backwardness. I honestly felt that what I was doing was patriotic, just like the things they do in these public relations offices we've set up in Europe and America. So why was I punished?

People call me 'the broker', *al-muta'ahhid*. I don't know who gave me the name, but I don't see why it should be considered an insult. I don't know if my work brings people happiness or trouble. The main thing is that my real name's been lost; it's just melted away, gone for ever, and all that's left are the words 'Effendi' and 'Ustaz'.* Some people address me as 'Ustaz Muta'ahhid' or 'Muta'ahhid Effendi'. That makes me reflect a bit—as is my right, being a former primary school teacher and the writer of this chapter. The word 'Muta'ahhid' comes from a root meaning 'to take custody' or 'to undertake something', and what I undertook was to promote the welfare of people who didn't know the proper steps to take for themselves, or how to find their way through the maze of government departments. I'm a broker who unties knots, and when I find a way out of problems that have made people confused or miserable or afraid, I feel I'm as great as our folk heroes Zanati Khalifa or Adham al-Sharqawi (who, incidentally, was related to my grandfather). The only difference between them and people like me is that their heroes' weapons were the sword and the gun, whereas mine are intellect, alertness, sharp thinking and the ability to unravel the knottiest problems.

* Effendi: a respectful title placed after the first name of a man, usually from the middle classes, when addressing him. Ustaz: a title meaning 'mentor', often also used when addressing people with some education, especially those in the teaching profession.

My story should have been written up in books and sung to the accompaniment of a stringed *rababa* on those lovely moonlit evenings of long ago which will never return to Egypt. I've achieved a great deal, and my one satisfaction in life is to succeed in what I do for others. I realize now that if I hadn't done these things for people, I'd have lost my reason for living. I'm telling you frankly what I've done, without hiding a thing. I can get identity papers for people who were never born, arrange marriages between people who've never heard of each other, sell land that exists nowhere but in the next world, move the boundaries of fields and get people's signatures on documents when they don't know what's in them—there are lots of things I can do. But what I like best of all is deals involving military service and everything that goes with it.

Every time I finished a job I hoped it would be the last, but as soon as I'd pulled it off, I'd get mixed up in something new, though what with all the dangers involved, I never knew how the next one would turn out. But why am I talking about all this? I think it's because I feel like crying; I'm feeling sorry for myself and I want your sympathy.

Anyway, the trouble's over now. A few months ago, the officer from my district who'd started it all came to see me; he was living with his relatives now. He'd come to congratulate me, he said; a new law had been passed, according to which anyone who'd been dismissed from his post other than through the normal disciplinary procedure would be getting his job back. He suggested we file a joint appeal; after all, we were both victims of the former regime. I told him to be patient and reminded him of our forefathers' advice: 'sow in haste, repent at leisure.' Why not wait and see how similar cases were decided before we lodged an appeal? That way we'd be sure.

Things improved, and I actually had more work than before, because everything was more relaxed and everyone was doing just as he liked. A helpful friend in Alexandria suggested we widen our field of action, because we might never get another chance. This is the first time in the history of the Nile Valley that Egyptians have been really free. Every Egyptian can do as he likes now. If he wants to travel, he travels; if he wants to run away, he runs away. Abu Zayd's path is open* and every path leads to whatever you want, as long as you have the money to pay for it. If you've got a piastre, you can get whatever a piastre buys.

I know the main reason you're reading this is to find out how the umda's problem turned out, and I'm sorry to have bothered you with things you're probably not interested in. But I wanted to get it off my chest. The mountains themselves couldn't bear the weight of the worries that press down on me night and day.

Let's come back to the business of the umda's son. After the umda left, I sat there reflecting on what he'd said about his land being returned, and that cheered me up and gave me confidence that I'd get my job back. Once that happened, I decided, I'd give up all these shady activities, and I vowed that what I did for the umda's son would put the last, crowning touches to my career as a broker.

I went straight to the district administration. The

---

* Abu Zayd, the hero of the folk tale of the Banu Hilal tribe, was renowned for his ability to find a way out of scrapes and dangerous situations.

way out of some problems is clear right from the start, while others are almost impossible to disentangle. With this one I was on familiar ground. I met a lot of people on the way. People's feelings towards me were ambiguous at that time; they didn't gloat the way they had when I'd lost my job, but I wasn't a hero for solving their problems either. Some said I might end up as a headmaster.

When I reached the administration building I went into the recruiting office, stood before the officer and winked. Then I went and waited outside, but he didn't come out—I suppose he didn't see me properly. I went back in, and this time he noticed me and followed me out. We went behind the office building and sat under a eucalyptus older than the offices themselves, along the bank of a small canal that watered nearby plantations. The officer told me how pleased he was to see me. 'Welcome, Ustaz,' he said.

That 'Ustaz' made me happy, because it seemed another good omen. We sat there facing each other; then he looked round carefully and asked me to come straight to the point. While I told him about the umda's son, he looked up at the sky, but didn't say anything. Finally he got up and threw down the matchstick he'd been using to pick his teeth. He smiled, the smile became a laugh, and he went into the old routine: how dangerous it was and how we might get caught. I heard him out and then told him what he wanted to hear—that he was clever enough to solve any problems that might crop up. It was going to be a battle of wits, I knew, and he was preparing the ground for getting as much money as he could. I decided to play on his greed, and I baited the hook. 'It's the deal of a lifetime,' I said.

We were both holding our own. His face relaxed

45

and then, after a moment's hesitation, he sat on the ground and the game of cat and mouse began. He went round and round the subject without saying a word about what was really on his mind—the money!

'Let's get down to brass tacks,' I said.

'It's all the same to me,' he replied.

He was afraid, he went on, that the affair might grow, with other people coming in on the deal. It ought to be dealt with at district level: there was no need to involve Alexandria or Cairo. As far as the actual arrangements went, half would be carried out in the district administration and the other half by the umda himself. This was surprising. I opened my mouth to speak, but he cut me off before I could say a word. 'I'm the only one who's a government official,' he said.

As the recruiting officer, he went on, he was right in the firing-line, and his position would make him the target of any suspicions. If the boat foundered everyone would get safely to shore except him, so he was going to prepare the boat himself. He stressed that I'd be doing everything through him.

It was true that I'd be working outside the main arena, but that was no reason to put myself at his mercy by ceding him all the initiative. It was too early to talk about money, I said. I wanted an assurance that he'd be able to deliver the goods, then we could talk about other things.

He came so close I could feel his breath on my face. 'It's always better to get the conditions sorted out beforehand,' he said. 'Let's make a deal first.' Then he started talking about thieves who got caught because they were seen quarrelling over how to divide the loot. I didn't know what to say. It seemed complicated, and I'd had doubts right from the start. Then I heard him say: 'I'll give you my answer in forty-eight hours.'

I was happy to hear that, and agreed to discuss it with him again in two days' time. Then I left and went on my way, dreaming of the day I'd be restored to God's grace, and He'd forgive me for this hateful work I do. When I'm working on a job, my whole life is a race in which I'm pursued by fear and the threat of the law, but once I've brought it off a thousand people come out of nowhere, all claiming they've helped me and wanting their cut. Then there are the blackmailers. 'Our country's welfare is at stake,' they say, 'and it's our patriotic duty to report this matter to the authorities.' 'All right,' I answer, 'I'll give you something to keep quiet.' So in the end all I get is a few millims, and it's a long time between payments, so what I earn when I do get paid isn't enough to settle all the debts I've accumulated. On top of this there's the daily fear, the need to cover up what I'm doing, the spectre of prison, the thought of disgrace . . . I could take all this for myself, but what crime have my children committed?

If I told you I had a guilty conscience, you'd laugh and say I was trying to make you feel sorry for me, but I swear I wouldn't do this sort of thing if I wasn't so badly off these days. Besides, half my work's standing up for downtrodden people. It's true the umda's son wasn't the victim of injustice, and in fact I don't feel very good about the job, but I needed the money. The umda's son should do his military service, as a matter of duty. If it had been my own son I'd have taken him to the door of the recruiting office myself, and come home proud and happy that he was serving his country.

The umda came to me at a bad time, when we didn't have much to eat. None of you really understands the saying 'Hunger makes a man blaspheme' —especially if you're reading this sitting in an armchair in a modern apartment, your stomach crammed with food, drunk from over-eating. Good, rich food makes you drunk, just like wine, so you won't believe me when I repeat: 'Hunger makes a man blaspheme.' But I'll say it again to myself when you're out of earshot, and I'd like to make it clear that I never got my pension, because I was sacked.

Anyway, let's get on with the story. The second time I met the recruiting officer behind the administrative offices, at the pre-arranged time, he seemed in a better frame of mind. He offered me a cigarette, laughed and told me he'd been thinking about the umda's son over the past two days. It certainly wasn't easy, but for my sake and the sake of the poor people who flock to us when they've got problems, he'd do what was necessary. The umda's son wouldn't have to do his military service, but we'd need the co-operation of the official in charge of the Civil Registry Office, someone in the Health Office, and some people from an agency with access to the official government stamp—we'd need two people there, plus their immediate superior. This worried me, because with all these people involved, there'd be hardly any pickings left for me. I asked if we couldn't get down to business. He looked carefully all around, then suggested we move away from the offices. Taking me by the hand, he led me away from the wall. 'Walls have ears,' he said.

We sat in the middle of a plot of watercress, the smell of the green leaves all around us. Then he started talking. The shortest distance between two points, he said, is a straight line. There was a quick, easy way to sort out the business of the umda's son, and there'd be no problem for an umda in carrying out the plan.

'So what's the plan?'

'Don't be in such a hurry,' he said calmly.

It was all so simple. His honour the recruiting officer started to explain his plan, whose most important feature was that it was absolutely foolproof. We set out for my house, where he asked for a pencil and paper and outlined the plan from A to Z. He wrote down a number of large headings: first, the stages of implementation; second, the participants in the operation; third, the expenses. All this was a general outline.

After he left, I sat there with his scribbled outline, and before I knew it (idleness affects people in strange ways) I'd picked up the pencil and started writing. It all seemed straightforward enough, and I found myself using my lazy brain for the first time in years. I got so engrossed in my work that a few hours later I had a whole pile of papers in front of me, with everything clearly set down, and in beautiful handwriting too. The papers covered the entire plan, and if you have no objection I'd like to include them here, so you can witness the great talents of one of the sons of Egypt, lost to the country through no fault of his own.

I. Stages of Implementation

A stage of implementation is a complete unit involving different steps, these steps being arranged in sequence, the success of each leading to the next, just as the disclosure of one of them would lead to the discovery of the others. The relationship between one stage and another is organic and complementary. One stage may include more than one step, and the safety of the whole plan depends on the successful execution of each of its parts.

The First Stage, Entitled 'The Replacement': As the title indicates, this stage involves the procedures concerning the person who is to be recruited in place of the umda's son, beginning with the requirements for this person and ending when the replacement is ready to play his appointed role. It is essential that the replacement fulfil the following conditions:

1. He must agree to be drafted as the umda's son, not merely as a replacement for him.

2. He must be born in the same village and on the same day as the umda's son.

3. He must himself be exempted from military service, so that there will be no second term of military service in his own name, which would expose the whole affair.

4. He must agree to hand over to us all the papers giving proof of his existence: for example, his identity card, draft card, election voting card and any personal or transport pass. These papers should be kept in a safe place by us or by the umda.

5. It would be advisable for him to be neither from a large family nor from a small family related to a large one. He must not have any common interests with the umda or one of the umda's allies. We must ensure that there is no connection of any kind between him and the umda's enemies anywhere in the district.

6. We must obtain, made out in the name of the replacement, a certificate of death from natural causes, preferably from some illnesses he actually

suffers from and which the whole village knows about. Moreover, since a small fee will ensure the co-operation of someone in the Health Office of the district administration, we will not confine ourselves to a simple, straightforward death certificate; the Health Office employee himself, in his official capacity, should also make a statement as to the circumstances of the death. The statement will contain words to the effect that the replacement suddenly fell ill and, there being no doctor in his village, was taken to the district hospital, where he died. A contagious disease was suspected and the necessary autopsy carried out, after which, to facilitate future re-examination of the body without offending the susceptibilities of simple-minded peasants, he had been buried near the hospital. His family was not to be informed of his death so as to prevent rumours, this being a critical time for our beloved Egypt, surrounded by enemies.

7. Having summoned the replacement's father, we must get him to give us a receipt for the sum paid to him, together with promissory notes; we must also issue forged cheques in his name for large sums of money, which could be used against him in the future. This will ensure his silence till his son leaves the army and will guarantee that he will testify on our behalf if the business is discovered.

8. We must inform the replacement that he is now the umda's son and that, to avoid any suspicion, he should conduct himself accordingly. To this end we must familiarize him with the umda's family history, possessions and associates, and with close family secrets known only to the umda.

The Second Stage, Entitled 'The Original': This involves all measures and procedures pertaining to the umda's son. He must leave the village and cease to attend any kind of educational establishment, since his appearance in the district or anywhere else in the province would lead to discovery of the plan. From the time the replacement is recruited, the original will officially be in the army, and in fact it will generally be believed that he is. It would be as well for him to have plastic surgery, to make sure he's not recognized at some chance meeting. The safest thing would be for him to go abroad under an assumed name, but if the umda refuses to accept this he must be hidden away somewhere in Egypt.

The Third Stage: The third stage has no title, being based on the interaction between the first and second stages. In fact, this stage involves the implementation of the whole operation, and reaching it implies that each party understands his role and the necessary precautions, so that all that remains is the careful application of the overall plan. At this stage an identity card will be issued bearing the full name of the umda's son together with a photograph of the replacement. The replacement will take this card to the district administration to obtain his call-up papers and travel form, and will then present himself at the recruiting office in Alexandria as the umda's son.

The composite identity card—bearing one person's name and another's photograph and fingerprints—will be issued by the head of the Civil Registry Office in the district administration, and it is on the issuing of this card that much of the success of the operation depends. It then remains to oversee the respective travel arrangements. The replacement will go to the Alexandria district, where we must keep him under close observation for the first few days; we must be sure that his behaviour is appropriate in every detail, since any error would lead to exposure of the whole plan. Meanwhile the umda's son will have to be sent as far away as possible, and we must make sure that he does not become known in any community, enrol in any educational establishment or participate in any commercial transactions. This situation must be maintained till the period of military service is safely over. *The Fourth Stage*: For the moment the fourth stage is a matter of probabilities only—the exact procedure cannot possibly be known till the game has reached its climax. At that decisive, dangerous moment when the referee claps and blows the final whistle, we shall have reached a new stage—known, under the rules of the game, as the reorganization of the opposition. At this point, the umda's son must return to the village as an honourable citizen who has discharged his military service; he must have a certificate declaring that he is a good Egyptian who has done his duty for his beloved country; he must wear dozens of medals and decorations won during the period of military service.

As for the replacement, he will take back all the papers that prove his existence in this world of ours (these being kept by us throughout his military service). He will then have three choices. First, he can return to the village as someone who volunteered for military service at the same time as the original was recruited to do his. But having seen how difficult life was in the army, he had decided not to spend the rest of his life in uniform and had refused to sign on for a new term. Preferring personal freedom to the chance of becoming an officer, he had answered the call of the Egyptian countryside, with all its peace, tranquillity, and human warmth.

His second choice is to go abroad, in which case we would provide all the necessary facilities.

The third is to obtain employment like anyone else released from military service. All he would have to do is give his unit a false place of residence, and so be assigned to another town. But this would involve a slight problem—the appointment will be in the name of the umda's son. How will the replacement be able to take up his job when he's just about to reassume his own identity? In fact, there's an easy way out. Either the umda's son will resign from the job in favour of someone else who needs it more and has been after it—in which case he will officially hand over the job to the replacement—or, alternatively we shall take the necessary steps to ensure that the appointment is in the replacement's name. Thus each party will return safely to his home base and the whole business will be brought to a happy conclusion.

II. *Participants in the Operation*
  1. The broker.
  2. The recruiting officer.
  3. The recruiting officer's aide.
  4. The director of the Civil Registry Office at the district administration.
  5. The Civil Registry Office official responsible for the issue of identity cards.
  6. The police officer responsible for taking the fingerprints of applicants for identity cards.
  7. The Health Office orderly who determines the applicant's blood group.
  8. The official responsible for issuing death certificates and burial permits at the District Health Office.

9. The military orderly responsible for escorting conscripts from the district town to the Alexandria recruitment zone, and then for handing them over to the authorities there.

10. A liaison officer who will keep the replacement under observation in the early days of his enlistment. This person will be in daily contact with the replacement, receiving detailed information as to how things are going, and instructing him on the appropriate behaviour at all times. In view of his easy access to the enlistment zone, it is suggested that the recruiting officer himself should undertake this important task.

11. A supervisor who will keep an eye on the umda's son, making sure he carries out his instructions after the replacement has gone for military service.

III. Expenses of the Operation

1. 100 (one hundred) pounds to arrange for the issue of an identity card bearing the photograph of the replacement and the name of the umda's son.

2. 150 (one hundred and fifty) pounds to obtain a death certificate for the replacement, dated prior to the day he begins his military service, together with a detailed report as to the circumstances of his death.

3. 20 (twenty) pounds to be paid to the district official who is responsible for fingerprinting, and who will take the replacement's fingerprints for his identity card and draft card.

4. 45 (forty-five) pounds for the orderly detailed to take charge of the recruits on the journey to

Alexandria. This is especially important, as he will be the first person to have any dealings with the replacement as the umda's son.

5. 60 (sixty) pounds for a friend employed in the Alexandria recruiting zone. This person will help supervise the replacement during the first days of his enlistment. He will provide moral support for the replacement, and guidance as to appropriate behaviour, and he will also warn us of anything which might lead to the plot being discovered. He will be our direct channel of communication with the replacement.

6. 300 (three hundred) pounds for the recruiting officer, since he will be directly in the firing-line.

7. 300 (three hundred) pounds for the broker, as he is in charge of the whole operation and in direct contact with the umda.

Comments

1. Any sums to be paid to the replacement and his family are not included in the list of expenses above, since they do not form part of the agreement. It has been made clear to the umda that he himself is solely responsible for finding the young man selected as the replacement.

2. The umda will bear any expenses incurred by his son during the period of military service, when, as a precaution, the young man will be living away from the village. This is because there is no knowing how many years the order relating to military service will remain in force.

3. The above list does not include costs incurred for transport, lodging and living expenses during the execution of the various stages of the plan.

This was the end of the memorandum.

The recruiting officer had told me from the start that it would be an extensive operation. At the time, I thought he was just saying this to trick me, but now I saw all the various aspects. The recruiting officer had dealt with everything on his side, and the fat was in the fire. The rest would be up to the umda and myself.

Next day I went to see the umda on my own. I knew where he lived and, getting out of the car at the banks of the canal, I set off for his house, being greeted along the way by people who knew me. I came across many of the young men of the village, and studied their faces with special care, wondering which one would be chosen as the replacement and have to present himself at the district administration to be sent off for military service as the umda's son.

The umda received me in his dawar, where he was sitting in judgement on the various cases and problems of his people. I was surprised at his limp handshake and lukewarm greeting, but he soon motioned to one of the night-watchmen to show me into the house, and from this man's respectful attitude towards me, it was clear that entry to the umda's house was a rare privilege. When he joined me inside, the umda became a different man, embracing and kissing me and apologizing for his cool reception of me in the dawar. He'd had to act like that, he said, so as not to draw attention to himself in front of all those people.

We chatted for a while, and he listened as I put forward the plan, presenting it as my own creation. His reaction was pure astonishment, and he sat there for a long time, thinking and gazing up at a small patch of sky visible through a window set high in the wall. Finally he said how ridiculous it was that I was unemployed these days, and added, pointing a fleshy finger at me, that Egypt would stay under-developed as long as most intelligent Egyptians weren't allowed to help develop the country. The crux of the matter was that those in power were afraid of clever people and the sons of good families. Plotting to keep me unemployed couldn't be doing Egypt any good.

He was generally happy with the plan, he said, although he had some reservations. First, there was no need to bind the replacement's father by demanding written security, since there was no danger of his betraying us, and in any case he wouldn't be giving up his son on this important mission for nothing. Besides, they were bound by a good many important and lasting interests. Second, there was the question of his son's going abroad; he was against this, and spent a long time arguing the point. He'd be quite frank, he said. He couldn't send the boy a long way off on his own because his mother couldn't bear to have him out of her sight for a moment. He was her only child and, for private family reasons he couldn't go into, things were going to stay that way. If the boy went to live so far away, his mother would insist on going with him, which would mean setting up house in a strange place—and there were various reasons, psychological, material and moral, why he'd find this difficult. We discussed the matter at length, neither of us budging, my arguments being based on the success of the plan and his on emotion. I finally persuaded him to accept my idea, and he agreed to send his son off somewhere with his mother. Next day, or in two days at the latest, he'd send the replacement to see me along with his father, and then we could get down to business.

Finally we came to the most important point: money. It would be advisable, the umda said, for me to take charge of the whole business, and he'd give me a lump sum at the end. This, of course, was a hint that he wanted some kind of guarantee. They all take that line. 'How can we be sure that the plan will work?' they ask. 'You really can't expect me to pay you everything now. Just go ahead, and when it's all over I'll give you everything you ask and more.'

In other cases this kind of talk might be reasonable enough, especially if the job was a small one, but this really did involve a lot of money; there were too many people in on the act and none of them would lift a finger before their palm was greased. I explained all this to him, but I could see he was still reluctant, so I told him bluntly that we'd never get started till we had enough money to cover at least the preliminary steps.

He complained that the plan was too expensive, especially since there were some things, like finding the replacement, that he'd have to take care of himself. 'You've none of you any idea how much that'll cost me,' he grumbled. And then there was the cost of setting his son up in some other household.

The discussion ended inconclusively, and he asked me to give him two days to think it over before we went any further. In that case, I said firmly, there was no point in sending the replacement to see me yet, because we wouldn't get anywhere without the money.

I was so furious I felt like murdering this unfathomable creature sitting opposite me, but when the servant brought in the lunch-tray his whole manner changed and he became the perfect host: generous, courteous and amiable. People really can be quite extraordinary, especially Egyptian country folk. 'We belong to the same family,' he remarked while we were eating. 'I've felt for a long time that there's a special kind of intimacy between us.'

He begged me to side with him and not with the people carrying out the arrangement; if I could cut down on their expenses, he said, he'd give me a commission on every pound I saved. I agreed, happy in the realization that the plan was now on, and I left on the understanding that we'd meet again in a couple of days.

3
The Night-Watchman

There's a proverb in our village: 'A couple of blows on the head and a man has such a headache he can't tell right from left.' That's what they used to say in the good old days, but now it seems you need just half a blow, even one little tap, and you can't stand up any more. Just look at what happened to me today.

First let me introduce myself. I think it's time to tell my part of the story, which believe me will stay with me to the grave and be buried with me in my heart— though I know well enough how narrow the graves of poor people like us are.

If I remember right, it all started with a knock at the door—just the kind of ordinary little tap that happens a thousand times in a night. Poor people bolt their doors at sunset to protect themselves from prying eyes, since no one ever comes to visit them or ask for favours. It was evening when the knock came, and I'd left the dawar and the storehouses I guard for the umda and gone home for supper. People are still awake at this time of the evening, so there's plenty of noise, and the lighted shops and houses give you a feeling of companionship, apart from keeping the night prowlers at bay.

I'd just put the first piece of bread in my mouth, but it was so dry it stuck in my throat and I couldn't eat. I motioned to them to take away the low table with the food on it and make me a big glass of tea, and my wife gave me a long, quiet look like the stagnant water in a drainage canal where nothing's stirred for years. I knew what that look meant—there was no sugar in the house. She got up and went to borrow some from a neighbour to tide us over till the next month's rations. I was furious.

The knock on the door reminded me of all the many blows I'd suffered recently. I'll start with the first, which I took as a deliberate attack, even though I knew perfectly well it was coming: I was pensioned off. I was a regular watchman right up to the legal retirement age, and then the district administration sent me a short letter—two copies, in fact—about the size of the palm of your hand. The post office clerk pressed his rubber stamp into the ink pad, stamped his copy and gave me the other, telling me I'd be a pensioner from the first of the month. I knew what was going on all right, because the same thing had happened to several friends of mine over the past few years. It was the end of going out at night to stand guard at the police station; and of being given my dear old rifle with the ten bullets, and doing the rounds of the lanes and alleyways with the gun slung over my shoulder, on nights that could be as cold as a lump of ice or as hot as a furnace; and of sleeping on stone benches near the outside walls of houses and shouting out 'Who goes there?' in the quiet, lonely nights. I wondered if I'd ever again be called by the proud title of *Shaikh al-Khafr*—head watchman.

Day and night I used to complain to the dirt on the ground about how hard my job was, but I missed it when they retired me, and my income fell dramatically. The nine and a quarter pounds I used to get now dropped to three and three-quarters, and this affected my standard of living and what I could buy and the way people treated me—the grocer wouldn't give me credit any more. But these weren't the only ways I suffered. The fact is, I'd been the oldest watchman in the village, so I'd been due for promotion to head watchman if the present head had been pensioned off or sacked, or had died. Now, feeling useless and horribly poor, I spent all my time in my field, whether there was anything to do there or not. I would have liked to spend the nights there too, but that would have cost too much, because it would have meant making separate suppers for the house and the field, and there would have had to be two pots of tea and two breakfasts instead of one. So I ate at home no matter how late I got in.

One winter's day I was walking past the umda's dawar, and the umda himself was sitting outside in the winter's sun, a sun as delightful as the most expensive out-of-season fruit. He called me over and asked how I was, and how my children and the household were doing. Then, when I complained about how bad things were, he gave me a job guarding his dawar, his livestock, his storerooms and his orchard.

'But that's the job of the watchman on duty in the telephone room,' I objected.

'I know it's always been his job', he said, 'right from my great-grandfather's day, but times have changed. These things are all the umda's private property now, so I have to pay to employ a watchman myself.'

One of the people sitting with him piped up—one

of those hypocritical hangers-on who do nothing but agree with everything he says as if they were parrots, and act for him in everything that goes on in the village. 'The umda's trying to help you,' he said, 'and he's such a kind, understanding man he doesn't want to hurt your feelings by offering you charity. His property lies within the village boundaries, and officially it's the special responsibility of one of the watchmen at the police station to take care of it. But the umda represents the government, so guarding his interests is the same as guarding the government.' It was my duty, the hanger-on concluded, to kiss the hand that was held out to me.

Next day I took up my new job. Even before, I was no stranger to the umda's household, but now I was the guard attached to his private residence. We hadn't come to any agreement over wages—I simply went to work on the umda's orders—but the kindness and generosity his youngest wife showed me made up for that. She'd send me breakfast and an evening meal, as well as tea and sometimes tobacco too. This was some consolation for the lean times we were going through.

That night the umda's wife didn't send me any food, and when I asked after her they told me she was ill. I said a prayer for her recovery, and when I went home for supper it occurred to me that perhaps she wasn't really ill but worried about something. She'd grown so pale recently she looked like one of us poor people. Her eyes wandered and she never stopped coughing. She was, as they say, going into a decline, though I didn't know just what the trouble was or what had caused it. In our village the poor are hidden behind their walls, and the secrets of the rich are no business of ours.

That knock at the door reminded me of all the knocks I'd taken recently. Some of them had been real blows on the head—they'd made me feel as if my life was over, and wish that death would come and release me.

I'd heard shots of celebration coming from the umda's dawar, and that made me happy, because here in the village we feel that the happiness of one is the happiness of all. It never crossed my mind that there were crucial times ahead, and that one man's joy would spell grief and ruin for another.

The shots had come from a rich man's house, which wasn't surprising, because life's just one long round of celebration for those people. But when my son came home, I saw a worried look on his face that I'd never seen before.

But before going into all that, let me introduce my son. His name's Masri, and he's my only son, the only boy among five girls. He's educated—he has a certificate from the village preparatory school—but that's as far as I could let him go, because any further studies would have meant paying for a place to live in the district town, and money or food, clothes and books too. Besides, someone has to help me in the field, and we need another man in the house. I'm getting old and we've got to have a man in the house to take my place.

Masri was determined to carry on with his studies. He always came top of his class, and the rich men's sons actually used to come to our humble home to study with him. We quarrelled about it, and Masri was about to leave home when we finally reached a compromise. He'd live at home, but catch up on the lessons from the students who went to the secondary school in the district town every day. Despite this disadvantage, Masri passed all his exams, coming first again.

Now he came in with anxiety written all over his face. I asked him about the celebrations, the cries of joy, the rifle shots.

'This is the blackest day of our lives,' came the astonishing reply. 'Today a decree's been issued ordering the return of the land that was taken from the umda and distributed to the peasants under the land reform. The police are going to take the land from the people it was given to and hand it back to the umda.'

At first I thought this meant just a change of ownership, with the umda taking over from the Land Reform Agency, but Masri quickly straightened me out on that. The umda, he said, with a bitter laugh, had told everyone who went to congratulate him that he wasn't going to take over even a hand's breadth of land if there was a tenant on it. He wanted no tenants, so he'd be free to do as he liked with the land— farm it, build on it, rent it out or have it worked by share-croppers.

I let me eyes wander over my field, a square patch of land, just three feddans, which had been mine for I don't know how many years. I looked at the animals' shed and the irrigation system, which my neighbours and I had built together as joint owners, and the eucalyptus tree, and the casuarina hedge bordering the land.

We both felt weak and helpless, especially Masri, who'd always been stronger than me but now seemed completely bewildered. I didn't know what to do, but I wanted to look like a fearless man of action in front of Masri, so I told him it was just idle gossip spread by people who had nothing to do, that nobody could take our land away from us. Finally Masri agreed that there was no power in all of Egypt that could do it.

He left me and went to the top of the field, where he sat with his feet in the canal and started throwing clods of earth into the water, watching the ripples spread out into ever bigger circles till they broke on the bank.

There was work to be done. It was late spring, there was a breath of summer in the air, and the fields were ripe for harvest. This is the best time of year—there's so much to be done that when I start work in the morning, I feel there just aren't enough hours in the day to finish everything. But now, looking at Masri and the field, I'd somehow lost interest. I picked up my hoe and sickle and hid them under a tree, then went to the irrigation trough and washed my face and feet with some stagnant water, leaving my face to dry in the twilight air. I hadn't said my prayers all day and thought about saying them now, but I was too confused and upset. The animals in the shed—the buffalo, the cow, the donkey and the sheep—seemed like orphans.

Masri and I headed for home—we were earlier than usual. It was a strange feeling, because usually I don't leave the field until the evening darkness comes, and I somehow felt that the trees and water courses and patches of bare brown earth were reproaching me for leaving them so soon.

It was difficult to get past the umda's house because of the crowd. One of the watchmen stopped us and pressed us to have a drink—a red sherbet smelling of acacia flowers—but Masri pushed him away. They almost had an argument, but the watchman was in a party mood and finally just laughed at us for refusing the umda's hospitality.

67

We realized what had happened when we got home and a group of peasants arrived. They were tenants of the Land Reform Agency too, and they'd heard about the decision against us. It was a judgement by default, because none of us had been summoned to court. The umda's case was against the government, so what did it have to do with us? We weren't regarded as parties to the case. Some people were sure we had the right to appeal against the decision, but someone else said we shouldn't rush into things. It was better to wait till the umda had his copy of the decision and started acting on it; as soon as that happened we could all start moving together. One hand can't clap on its own, he said, and we had to stick together. But a widowed peasant woman with several children to support said, 'Water never flows uphill. The umda will take the land whatever we do.' That made Masri really angry. 'He's not going to get it,' he said. 'We'll defend the land with our lives if we have to.'

Next day the news that the umda's land was about to be returned was the talk of the village. In this atmosphere rumours were rife, and they all amounted to very much the same thing—the umda was determined to get his land back.

The knock at the door gave me a real fright. We'd now spent three days in fear and expectation. People kept saying that it takes for ever and a day for the government to carry out its decisions and that it would take at least three years for the umda to get a copy of the order. But in fact he'd sent for a car the very day the decision was announced and set off for the district town with the telephone room clerk. Everybody said he'd soon be back with a copy of the decision, and he'd act on it the next day.

My neighbour said he'd seen the umda when he came back, but he didn't have the copy with him. In fact he'd seemed anxious and bewildered, as if burdened with all the cares in the world.

On the third day a police officer arrived with three men, all on white police horses. We're always afraid when they come to country areas like this. The officer summoned all the tenants of the land that was due to be restored to the umda, and when we were all assembled, we met him in the umda's dawar, in the room where the weapons are kept. The officer told us that the courts had decided that our land should be returned to the umda. It was his land really, because it had belonged to him at the time of the expropriation, before it had been rented out to other people; so it must be returned to him without sitting tenants. Anyone who'd had a rent agreement with the umda before the land was confiscated could carry on renting it, but all agreements drawn up by the Land Reform Agency were null and void, and the land had to be returned to the umda immediately. The officer said that, as a policeman, he was very conscious of being an Egyptian and our kinsman, and that was why he'd wanted to give us the order at a friendly family meeting. If we obeyed the order, all well and good, but if not he'd have to enforce it.

His honour the officer didn't mince words. He said right out that the land would have to be given back to the umda, but added that he would appeal to the umda on our behalf and ask him to have pity on us. He didn't want to see us left with no land to farm, because we were kinsfolk and we should be able to live our lives in a spirit of love and brotherhood, not hatred and discord.

One of us stood and asked, 'What's going to

happen to us and our children?'

'God will protect you,' the officer answered, 'and after God you have the umda. He'll be responsible for bringing your situation to the attention of the appropriate authorities, so that they can take action on your behalf. Egypt will never leave her sons without land or work. She's generous to foreigners, and you can be sure she'll be far more generous to her own sons.'

'It's tyranny!' shouted another peasant.

'We're dealing with a legal verdict that has to be carried out,' replied the officer sharply. 'As to whether the verdict is just or unjust, that will be decided by a tribunal, and these days—thank God! —the law is enforced. There is no voice higher than the law. It's our duty to act according to the judgement handed down. Any complaints should be made through the proper legal channels after the judgement has been implemented. Then, if your appeal's upheld, the land will be given back to you at once. Rest assured: I'll see that it's carried out.'

Thank God Masri wasn't there—I don't know what he would have done to the officer if he had been. The meeting turned rowdy, with people arguing and protesting, and the officer declared that his only concern was to see the decision carried out, and it would be better if the land was handed over amicably. He'd give us two days, he said. If people handed over their land without any fuss, then all well and good, but if anyone refused he'd apply the law and take the land by force. People started shouting at that, but the officer stiffened in his chair, then put on his cap and stood up. The soldiers who'd come with him saluted, and so did the watchmen standing around the gun-room. Then the officer went to see the umda, while we went out clenching our fists in despair. We couldn't agree among ourselves, and it looked pretty much as if the officer was deliberately giving us a chance to fall out with each other.

Some people said that if this was Egyptian justice they were going to emigrate. Here were the authorities, taking land away from people who had nothing, so they could give it to someone who had everything he could possibly desire. Others said it would be more honourable to sell the land and animals and buy weapons instead, even if we had to fight the government itself. We could be sure, one of them said, that if this had happened in Upper Egypt the officer would never have got away alive, even if he'd had the entire army with him. All this talk got us nowhere.

It was midday, but I didn't go out to join Masri in the field. When he finally came in with the animals at dusk, I'd spent the whole of the rest of the day by myself, going over and over everything. I didn't know what to do. I told myself that whatever happened to the others would happen to me too. And yet I was the umda's guard, who went to his house every evening, and that meant I had special ties with him. I decided not to go back till I found out how he was going to treat us all. When my wife saw my grave face, she said the umda would probably let us keep our land because I was his personal guard and he liked me. I yelled at her and wouldn't listen, determined to throw in my lot with the others whatever happened.

That was when the knock at the door came. The dog, who was asleep just behind it, woke with a start, gave a loud bark and tried to sink his teeth in the wood. I got up and opened the door. It was the watchman on duty in the telephone room, and he told me the umda wanted to see me urgently.

I didn't stop to think. I put on my slippers and was about to leave when my wife said that the tea was brewing, so the watchman joined me for a glass before we left. I thought the umda must want me to do some work in one of his fields, and he's sent for me to tell me about it before having an early night.

When I got to the dawar, I found the telephone-room clerk waiting for me. The watchman said he'd brought me to see the umda, and to my surprise the clerk asked me to sit down and then sent the watchman to bring us a pot of tea from the umda's house. He made room for me on the high couch where he was sitting, and when I hesitated he pulled me by the hand and had me sit down next to him. He started in a roundabout sort of way. The umda was a good man, he said; he'd done an enormous number of favours for the people in the village. There wasn't a single household where he hadn't done a good turn for somebody, but he had a special affection for me. 'However,' he continued, 'there's an old Egyptian saying that the eye of jealousy is always turned towards people higher up. Now the umda says you're different from all the other villagers, and that's why he's sent for you tonight, to ask you to do something very simple for him. He's quite sure you'll rally to the flag, because it's a favour that's well within your power.'

The whole thing was starting to make me nervous. Why was he beating about the bush like this? There's been an umda ever since we can remember, who was the son of the umda before him, and the descendant of other umdas before that. As for us, we were born to spend our lives bent over a hoe and to die with our

feet sunk deep in the earth, our backs permanently
bowed from the never-ending stoop. In fact bend-
ing's all we do all our lives. The umda's always given
instant commands—he points a finger and we do
what he says. Now I felt fear creeping over my body
like ants do if you fall asleep in the fields. I was going
to tell the clerk what I was thinking, but he just
talked on and never gave me the chance.

I stood up when the umda arrived, and then I saw
he was holding out his hand for me to shake. Now I
was sure something had happened. The government
must have annulled its decision about the return of
his land, I thought. I was happy; I felt a sudden surge
of longing for my land and had visions of myself
going there the next day with my animals. As I took
the umda's smooth, flabby hand between my own
hands—which were dry and full of cracks like
parched earth—I felt a pricking in my palm from the
stones in the rings on his fingers. I bent over to kiss
his hand. It was heavy and fat, warm and fleshy, and
as my lips buried themselves in the folds of flesh I
remembered I hadn't tasted meat since the last feast
day. I made a quick attempt to work out how many
months it had been since the last feast, but all this
counting of days and months was too much for my
tired brain. The umda left his hand where it was so I
could carry on kissing it—he imagines we like it
when he leaves his hand there long enough for us to
go on and on kissing it like that. I kept on kissing it,
and the umda said, 'May God forgive me, my son.'

He patted me on the back with his other hand,
then let it rest on my spine, and you could tell from
the weight that this was a hand that had been fattened
up by the rich life of the good old days. There's no
flesh on my hand, or on the hands of thousands like

me; but I was afraid he might hurt himself because my backbone's as sharp as a row of nails!

He finally took his hands away and went over to the couch. Then, to my utter amazement, he sat down, gathered up his great gown—which had enough material in it to clothe my entire family—and invited me to sit next to him! I picked up the hem of my skimpy gown and sat on the floor by the large couch, but he swore by the mercy of his dear departed that this would never do, pulled me up and had me sit down next to him. Then he motioned to dismiss everyone except the clerk. In front of us was a tray with a pot of tea and three large glasses with gold bands round them.

By now utterly bewildered, I was afraid of what was happening. I wished the two of them would say something to calm all the doubts and questions buzzing in my head like bees. They weren't honouring me like this for nothing—they wanted something from me. I was relieved when the courtesies were over and they got down to it.

What the umda was asking me to do, said the clerk, was both difficult and easy, complicated and straightforward at the same time; but it was in my power to do it. Was I willing? I replied that we were all at the umda's command, and after a short silence the clerk asked the umda to speak for himself; that way it would be clear he was asking a favour from me.

The umda cleared his throat, then put his hand in his pocket and took out a handkerchief as fine as cigarette paper. It filled the room with its fragrance. He spat into it and then cleared his throat again. This man, I thought, has always eaten his fill, and now his throat's so choked with eating that his voice comes out smelling of meat and chicken, butter and fried onions. Moving closer to me, the umda asked what I intended to do about the land. At last I felt I could relax, that we'd come to the end of all the twisting and turning, and I told him we hadn't decided what we were going to do. That word 'we' brought him up short. 'Who's *we*?' he asked.

I told him that 'we' were the peasants who were going to be driven off our land. We hadn't decided what action to take yet, but most people were in favour of resisting the officer by force if necessary. That didn't make him angry. He just laughed and said, 'Never mind the others; I'll treat you as a special case.'

'A man must keep his word,' I answered. 'In fact, he's only as good as his word. I've discussed it with my brother villagers and I have to stand with them . . .'

He interrupted before I could finish. 'I'm going to make you a special case,' he said, 'not just out of kindness, but because I've got a favour to ask you. What I'm asking you to do is to let Masri take on a simple job in place of my youngest son—the son of my youngest wife, the woman who gives you your supper and breakfast, and whom you love just as you love your own children. She, I might add, looks on you as a father. It will be enormously helpful if Masri can take on this job.'

The clerk got in on the act too. The umda, he said, expected me to make my son available, but of course every job has its price, and as soon as we came to a basic agreement we'd get down to details and I'd know exactly what I was going to get from the umda.

They filled me in bit by bit; it took half the night to go through it all. I could hear the usual chatter in the main street outside the umda's dawar: children were shouting and playing, men were betting, someone

75

was looking for a lost hen or a sheep that had wandered off on the way home from the field. One man was asking where he could find a peasant who owed him money, another was complaining he didn't have a millim to his name. In the midst of all this I calmly took in everything the two of them told me, point by point.

'What we're asking Masri to do', said the clerk, 'can be done in the twinkling of an eye. He'll go and collect some important papers from the district administration in place of the umda's youngest son, and then come back. The umda will pay all expenses.'

The umda himself added something the clerk had forgotten. Masri would pick up the papers from the administration—incidentally, they weren't important or of any value—then go on to Alexandria the same day, hand them over to someone there, and be back in the village by sunset. 'A simple task like that would be child's play for Masri', he said.

Once more I asked why the umda's son couldn't go, and why it was so important for Masri to go instead. That's when the first blow fell.

'Masri', said the clerk, 'will go as the umda's son.'

In a sudden panic, I asked what exactly the papers were.

'Oh, just call-up papers,' the umda answered with a wave of his hand, as if it was of absolutely no importance.

Before I could take it all in, the clerk was asking if I agreed, and I pointed to my head to show the turmoil my thoughts were in. The umda gestured to the clerk, and the clerk finally took the lid off the pot, as we say, and I got the full smell of the whole business. He ran through the story, getting so worked up that white flecks of spit flew out of his mouth. They settled at the corner of his mouth and on the end of his tongue at first, but then he increased the range so they reached my face and clothes. I got completely lost as I tried desperately to follow what the clerk was saying. Several times I begged him to stop so I could straighten things out in my mind, but he just cut me off, and I never did get to say a word. My jaw fell, my hands hung loose at my sides, and a big drop of sweat slid down under my clothes from neck to chest. I could feel it running through the hairs on my chest and then rushing down towards my stomach, getting colder as it went.

This is what the clerk said: 'Two days ago the order arrived for the umda's son, who's the same age as Masri, to go off to the army, to do his military service. Due to reasons and circumstances which would take too long to explain (and which would merely be painful to discuss), the umda doesn't wish his son to go. You'll be aware of some of the circumstances, since the umda regards you as one of his household; that's why he chose you specially to guard it. The umda's looked everywhere for a way out, but all the doors were slammed shut in his face—I'm sure you know what it means for a man to have every door shut in his face. If his son goes off to the army it'll wreck his household, and he'll lose everything he's worked so hard to build up. At last we hit on a simple, easy solution: someone else will go in his place. And since the umda feels you're closer to him than a brother, and looks on Masri as his own son, Masri will go into the army instead of his son. If you agree, the umda's prepared to discuss things with you; he'll give you whatever you ask, and he's a man who can do the impossible. The main thing is for you to agree to this simple little request. So how about it?

77

—what do you say?'

A heavy silence followed. 'I don't understand what you want from me', I said.

They looked at each other. The first signs of anger appeared on the umda's face, and the clerk begged him not to lose his temper. The simple favour they wanted from me—or rather from Masri—slowly sank in: my only son, born after a whole troop of girls, would have to go into the army in place of the umda's seventh son. They were pressing me for an answer, but I didn't say yes or no. I never make snap decisions when faced with a complicated problem, and I asked for time to think it over. They refused.

'If you're thinking of discussing it with someone and getting their views,' said the clerk, 'then forget it. That would be dangerous for the umda. I want you to answer yes or no, and either way the matter must remain totally confidential.'

'What about the person concerned?'

'Who do you mean?'

'Masri himself.'

'I don't follow you.'

The clerk then went on to say that Masri shouldn't be told everything all at once, but should be brought into it bit by bit. 'No one knows how he'll react when it's put to him,' he said. 'Young men these days are as deep as the ocean.'

'If I can just be alone for a bit,' I said, 'I'll think it over.'

They suggested leaving me on my own in the dawar, but I told them I'd rather put off my answer till the next day. 'It'll be all right,' I said. I don't know why I added that. It's my worst fault: sometimes words come out of my mouth and I don't really know what they mean. I was happy because I was going at last and they would leave me alone.

When I got up to go, the umda took me by the arm. 'There's got to be give and take in this world', he said, 'and a man who does a job gets his reward. But it doesn't matter whether you refuse or accept; I'll reward you anyway. We'll leave it to your conscience whether you want to say yes or no, but I'm sure you won't leave me in the lurch. How many feddans did you get from the Land Reform Agency?'

'Three,' I answered.

I went on to say that I had a lease with the Land Reform Agency which was registered with the Agricultural Co-operative Society. 'For five years now,' I said, 'they've been telling us that the agency would make us owners of the land, with the rent we've already paid counting towards the price. But time's gone by and our dreams haven't come true, and now this evening we've had the disastrous news that our land is going to be taken away from us.'

'You're one family now,' said the clerk, meaning me and the umda. The things I'd done for the umda, he said, made our two families 'one blood'.

The flattering lie made me laugh inside. After all, we've known since we were children that the umda has blue blood in his veins—the colour of a cloudy sky in winter. It smells of perfume too, not like the grubby red blood of people like us, who have full stomachs only in their dreams! Maybe the sarcasm showed on my face—anyway the clerk saw clearly enough what I was thinking. It really was true, he said, that our blood had become one, and he went on to explain that if Masri went into the army in place of the umda's son, it counted as a 'blood tax', and that was the greatest gesture of love that one of Egypt's sons could make for another. Nothing like it, he said, had ever happened before.

'Whatever happens,' interjected the umda, 'you'll never be driven from your land.' He repeated this three times, then he took out the Koran, whose pages he uses to keep ten-pound notes in—his wallet's full of them too, as crisp and sharp as knives! I only just managed to stop him swearing on the Koran.

As far as my land was concerned, he said, he'd cancel the tenancy agreement the Land Reform Agency had made, and that way people wouldn't talk. But I'd keep the land and I could farm it on a share-cropping basis; he'd provide the land, and my children and I would work on it all year, then we'd divide the harvest and expenses equally, except that the umda would deduct the rent for the land from the harvest. This rent wouldn't be paid once a year like everyone else's, but according to the crop, with the rent for planting cotton being different, for example, from the rent for planting clover.

'Let's work out how much you'll make,' the umda went on. 'Suppose a peasant sows a feddan widely. Let's say he forgets about the usual crops, ignores all the empty talk about the national economy, the good of the state, exports, and all the endless plans, and refuses to grow on a rotation basis. Well, he can make a thousand pounds a year from a single feddan if he plants fruit trees, and even the usual crops will bring in a cool six hundred. But let's be cautious and suppose you make only four hundred. Then let's allow for pests and drought, and the evil eye, and bribes to make things easier. We end up with two hundred pounds a feddan, so three feddans give you six hundred pounds. Over the period of Masri's military service you'll make one thousand eight hundred pounds—almost two thousand!—and I won't count the cattle or firewood or the food you get, because we're one family after all. If you do a really good job and make a success of things, maybe I'll give you other pieces of land later on. We won't ever write this agreement down. It'll stay a secret between us.'

He said that he would tell people that he was paying me a wage to work the land. In addition, guarding the dawar was a permanent job, paying ten piastres a night or three pounds a month, and since everything in the dawar was obviously safe, because no one would dare touch an umda's possessions, that meant I was getting three pounds a month for sleeping at the dawar instead of at home. Even so, bearing in mind the great favour I was going to do him, he'd double my wages for the job: twenty piastres a night, or six pounds a month, which was as much as the pension I was getting from the government. That meant, quite simply, that, including my pension, I'd have twelve pounds on the first day of every month, which was more than the salary of the government schoolteacher, the postmaster or the agricultural superintendent of the Co-operative Society, and less only than the salary of his honour the officer at the central police station, who ruled over loyal people like us.

To round off the calculations, he said—and he didn't begrudge me the money the way some jealous people might—there'd be seventy-two pounds a year going into my house (not counting my pension), which made two hundred and sixteen pounds over three years. If we added the income from the land, that made two thousand and sixteen pounds. Now, while Masri was in the army he'd be getting three pounds a month, and we might be able to work things cleverly so that he got an appointment allowance and clothing allowance after arranging, through a contact, to have him transferred to Military Intelligence. His pay there would be fifteen pounds a month, he'd get free food and transport, and he'd be able to further his interests and those of his family too. 'So,' the umda continued, 'we can expect him to get a hundred and eighty pounds a year, or five hundred and forty pounds over the whole period. Do a simple calculation, and you'll find you've got your hands on two thousand, five hundred and fifty-six pounds. It's now the end of June 1973, and if Masri goes into the army at the beginning of July, he'll be out at the beginning of July 1976. That's not very long in a man's life. It'll be over in the merest twinkling of an eye, before anyone even realizes he's gone.

'Suppose he doesn't leave the army on that date. If they ask him to stay on, and increase his pay from 1 July 1976, he won't be getting less than twenty pounds, and the pay can often reach forty pounds if the right contracts are made, or if he gets in good with the commanding officers, or if he uses his head like a good recruit and manages to get a lot of service ribbons, medals and decorations. This salary will be paid till he's discharged from the service, and the day that happens his unit commander will present him with various offers he can accept or refuse just as he likes.

'The first alternative will be for him to stay on in the army as a regular soldier. That's a higher status than a conscript's, with a salary of a full fifty pounds, and in five years he'll be commissioned as an officer, starting as second lieutenant. Masri's young, which means he'll be a general by the time he retires, with the same rank as the provincial chief of police. Just think of that! It's beyond anyone's wildest dreams!

'If, on the other hand, Masri decides not to stay in

the army—which he's perfectly free to do—he'll get an official letter from the administrative office of the Supreme Command of the Armed Forces, addressed to the place where he wants to find civilian employment.'

Actually, Masri's a true son of the soil, and I know he'd refuse any position they offered him in the city; he'd never agree to be a city governor, a prosecutor, a doctor or an engineer. He'd rather be a teacher in our village primary school, so he can pass on the light of learning to the poor, miserable country folk. Masri's suffered himself from being denied education, and because of that he'd be an even better bridge to bring enlightenment to the people.

'What's the pay for an administrative position in the government?' asked the umda.

I didn't answer. My mouth was dry; you could actually hear my heart pounding against my ribs.

It was the clerk who answered. 'It's equivalent to fifty feddans,' he said.

'One feddan of land costs two thousand pounds,' the umda went on, 'not counting the additional purchase fee, which amounts to the cost of a further half feddan. So the position's worth a hundred thousand pounds.'

After all, who was doing who the good turn?, he asked me. The clerk objected to this, saying the point was immaterial; the goal was the general good: the good of our village and the good of our Egyptian motherland.

There was a sudden silence. The clerk drew close to me and asked if I'd witnessed *Laylat al-Qadr** during

* *Laylat al-Qadr*: 'the night of destiny', was, according to the Koran, when the Holy Book was first revealed to the Prophet Muhammad. It is regarded as 'better than a thousand months' and a common belief holds that God will grant the wishes of any believer to whom it is revealed. It is believed to occur at the very end of Ramadan.

the recent month of Ramadan. If I had, he said, my good luck was understandable, but if I hadn't, then what was happening to me was a real miracle. What the umda had just told me could be called a miracle, because it involved aspirations beyond any man's wildest dreams. It was unbelievable that they could be fulfilled all at once, just like that.

'It never occurred to me', I replied, 'that Laylat al-Qadr had anything to do with poor people like me. From the earliest days of our forefathers, luck's always the bosom friend of the rich and powerful, of people who don't need it. We've never seen any of it.'

The clerk came up close again and asked me to open my mouth and raise my upper lip. Then he tilted my face so as to get a good look at my teeth, and remarked they weren't the lucky sort. Now if I'd been born with a wide gap between the two front teeth, that would have been a sign of indescribable good luck. The clerk seemed puzzled, but he was rescued by the umda, who slapped my thigh so hard the pain made me dizzy. Masri had teeth like that, he said. Hadn't he told me years ago, when Masri took his first steps, that the child was lucky? He swore he'd said then that the child had the world at his feet.

'Your honour said it was a lucky step,' the clerk corrected him.

'Yes, you're right. That's what I said.'

I couldn't remember him saying it, but it's true Masri does have a gap between his teeth, and a lot of people have remarked he was born lucky. I got up, saying I had to go, but the umda said I couldn't leave his house without supper, and he clapped his hands and the clerk went in to hurry the meal along.

Thank God I've been able to describe the conversation. I was afraid I wouldn't, because it was so difficult and complicated, and had the kind of big numbers I've never had to deal with. Have I told it right? Maybe not, but I've repeated what I was able to understand, and that'll have to do.

The servant came in with a tray on her head, a heavy brass tray with a cloth over it, the kind you see at rich men's funerals. When the umda lifted the cloth, steam rose from all the plates and bowls, and I could see the brown drumsticks of a goose or turkey sticking out. My mouth watered and my guts stirred, making me feel as if my stomach was as wide as the canal in my field and I hadn't eaten for years! When I saw what was on the tray, I realized it was no chance meal: this feast had been prepared in advance.

I sat opposite the umda with the clerk next to me, while a watchman, an old colleague of mine, stood by us holding a water jug, glass and towel. I was over-joyed at the sight of all this unexpected food—nobody had ever put anything like this in front of me before! There'd been times when I'd carried that same tray from the dawar back to the house after the umda's guests had eaten, and then I used to stop on the way, behind a door or near some wall, and eat the leftovers; or find some safe hiding place for them till I could take them home.

The umda said grace in a loud voice, and then we stretched out our hands to the food. There was a thing there called a fork; it looked like the tool we used to winnow wheat, but much smaller and made of metal instead of wood. Knives and spoons I already knew about. I've had a knife at home ever since I married Masri's mother, and the carpenter made us wooden spoons too, along with the chest and the little low table we eat off. I didn't know whether I could eat with my fingers or not. The umda

85

picked up a knife and fork and cut a piece off the goose or turkey or whatever it was. I was afraid. Perhaps the umda would get angry if I stretched out my hand. I wished they'd given me my share of the food so I could eat it alone, without all this horrible cutlery I felt like throwing out of the window! I put my knife and fork to one side, and ate what I could eat with a spoon: soup, rice, vegetables and salad. The umda had been acquainted with every kind of food for years and years—an intimacy I don't share. As he began his meal, cramming his mouth with meat, his face relaxed, and to look at him you'd think there was nothing he enjoyed more in the world.

After we'd eaten I said I really had to go, and the umda said he'd give me two days to think things over. The clerk reminded me I should tell Masri about everything little by little, and I promised to do this. Then I left, staring at the ground as I walked along, my back bent and finding it difficult to lift my feet. I didn't go home; instead I went to the umda's storehouse, where I thought about this business of Masri. It was through him and his affairs that I'd come to understand what went on in the world. When he was a child, all I knew about was the piece of dry bread I asked God to give me every day and I used to kiss both sides of the bread before eating it. At night, through the long, dark hours that went by so slowly, all I longed for was sleep, and in the morning I'd go to the gun-room to turn in my rifle, secretly praying the umda wouldn't see me on my way home, because if he did he'd send me to work in his great fields. All my life I've been hungry all day long: hungry for sleep, hungry for bread, hungry for clothing, hungry for rest—a lifetime of hunger. I tried to stop thinking about it, but I just couldn't.

Would I agree to send Masri to the army in place of the umda's son? 'Never,' I said.

I was surprised to hear myself say the word, but it didn't calm my fears about Masri. I'd been afraid from the moment I left the umda's house, and there was no escaping it. I decided to tire myself out, so that I'd be able to sleep later on, when I'd take the old, worn blanket that was as full of holes as a sieve, pull it over my face and ask sleep to come. When I slept I'd make the noises I used to hear everyone else making at night, when I was on duty.

Sleep has a fragrance I can smell. It divides people into two categories: the ones who get as much sleep as they want and the ones who don't. When I used to pass the mansions of well-off people on my nightly rounds, they always seemed to be in a deep sleep, and I was afraid my footsteps would wake them. It was true I was there to protect them against evil-doers, but I wasn't supposed to wake them.

That's how my working life was, and when I finally got my pension I thought I'd sleep for ever. I retired, and a few days later, there I was a watchman again, working for the umda. Then this business of Masri came up, and what sleep I had left was snatched from me; that's how I got all these deep lines on my face. Did I say face? Well, let me introduce you to this face. There are more than just warts. My eyes are always bloodshot—you don't have to get that close to see how red they are—my eyelids lost their lashes during the long, sleepless nights, and my nose drips endlessly, like a tap. You could even say my nostrils are more generous than the tap near our house, which hasn't given us a drop of water since they put it there.

That knock on the door had brought disaster. 'I

hope they'll be satisfied now,' I thought bitterly. Masri used to be the talk of the village. 'How can a poor man's son be so brilliant?' 'Where does he get his intelligence?' 'Who did he get a brain like that from?' A few days ago Masri's mother quoted the old saying: 'It's a strange sight, a cake in an orphan's hand.'

There's never been a case like Masri's, and when he got his preparatory school certificate I didn't know what to do. After all, education's the best thing there is, and people like me have always longed for one of our sons to come home one day as an educated man, an effendi. Masri was a bright pupil and his reputation spread throughout the village. He always came first, not only in his class but in the whole school. He'd come first ever since primary school, and his brains had a lot of important people knocking at my door, asking if I'd let Masri study with their sons so they'd sail through their exams. People used to explain it by saying that the poor are clever and the rich are stupid, but I never swallowed that. Rich man can afford to want things and then get what they want. They can be clever if they want, because their money's got the power to buy just as much intelligence as they need.

The day Masri got his preparatory school certificate, we had a problem. The only secondary school is in the district town, and the special schools for things like business and agriculture and teacher training are in the big city where the district chief of police and governor are. Masri and I quarrelled about his future. He wanted to study arts at the secondary school, then go on to university and eventually, God willing, actually become a teacher there. In my view, the best job in the world is to be a primary teacher at our village school, but Masri refused to consider it. He talked about higher education and intermediate education, and said he was willing to be a teacher as I wanted, but only after he'd graduated from the Faculty of Law or the Faculty of Arts. Of the two, he said, he'd prefer the former.

All this was over my head, and I looked at him in amazement. I was puzzled. Where had Masri learned about all these things? Although I wanted him to reach his goal in life, I discovered only too soon that it was impossible for him to go to school outside the village. He'd need a place to live, which would have to be furnished and have water and electricity, and he'd never be able to go school in the district town without expensive clothes. Then he'd need food, the fare to travel to and from the village once a week and money for exercise books, textbooks and pens. I was a poor man living from hand to mouth. It's true I farmed three feddans, had a watchman's salary and a share in two head of cattle, but I was responsible for supporting nine people besides myself: Masri, his five sisters, their mother, my mother and my mother-in-law. They were all there day after day, demanding food and clothing. Where could I find the money to set him up in the expensive district town, where the kohl's stolen off people's eyes and they even try and sell you the water and air? I was doing all I could already.

The villagers were concerned about Masri's future, and several men came and begged me to let him finish his studies in the district town. I replied in the words of an Arabic proverb: 'The eye can see,' I told them, 'but the arm is short.' What could I do? People were angry with me and said that God was powerful enough to do anything, but providence moves in mysterious ways, and earrings come to those without ears. Only God understands why things are the way they are.

One day when we were in the field, I called Masri over. 'You're the only son among five girls,' I told him, 'and I can't support you in the district town. One feddan of land is the equivalent of a steady job, and I rent three feddans, which one day will belong to us—they're rented now, I know, but I'm sure it won't be long before we own them. We've waited for more than twenty years and the day must come soon. And they'll all be yours, Masri, because your sisters' only aim in life is to get married. The land will be yours, and that'll be compensation for not continuing your studies. Let's find a respectable girl for you to marry, so you can build a little nest, even if it's only a poor man's nest.'

Masri looked me straight in the eye before he spoke, and it was as if he'd aged ten years in the short time I'd been speaking. He was angry, his eyes were brimming with tears and I could hear him gnashing and grinding his teeth. He told me he was going to carry on with his studies however he could, that he didn't know the meaning of the word impossible and that he wasn't born to till land he didn't own. He'd carry on with his studies at home, he said.

'At home!' I exclaimed.

His answer showed me what a huge gulf separated us. It was possible, he explained, to enrol at the secondary school in the district town even though he was based at home. He could stay here and study on his own, then take the exam at the end of the year. He was certain he could keep it up for three years.

That makes twice now that I've recorded this conversation with Masri, standing here guarding the umda's possessions with the gun the umda brought me (he paid for the licence too), and I really don't know why. I do my best to get away from the subject of Masri, but I can't get him out of my mind. Right from the start I didn't want to have anything to do with the whole thing, because the world and everything in it isn't worth the dust under Masri's feet, but as you can imagine, it wasn't easy to forget the umda's promises—especially about the land.

Yesterday I heard that land had already been given back to its old owners in a few places, and that the umda was going to get his back whether we liked it or not. I was hungry, and the umda's offer meant bread to fill my mouth, and the mouths of all my family as well. And so I hesitated, even though I was surprised to find myself doing so. When the umda had first spoken to me I didn't feel like even considering his offer, but after mulling it over—well, I hesitated. When night came I hesitated even more, and in the nights that followed I didn't sleep a wink. It all seemed like a dream. A strange sleeplessness I'd never known before came over me, and the long nights became endless. When the ghostly grey hour of dawn drew near, I'd feel my time of decision approaching, then at dawn a pale peace, a strange calm would descend on me. I'd go to the mosque, perform my ablutions, pray, tire myself out with thinking and decide to ask someone for advice; but fear of disgrace and what people would say made me keep my mouth shut. On the final morning I went back to hand over the umda's dawar and storerooms, which took a long time that day. Then I left and went home.

And now I come to the crucial part of the whole story—what happened between Masri and me when

I went home on that dreadful morning. Please forgive me: I know this is the vital thing you want me to tell you about, but nothing will ever make me repeat it. I just couldn't stand it. It's hard enough to even mention it, how could I betray Masri by giving the details? I know you'll be angry, and say I've been leading you on. I've only told you as much as I want to, you'll say, and then, when we get to the crucial part, I back off. Well, what happened between Masri and me on that fateful morning is no secret. Find out about it any way you want, but you'll never hear it from me.

I'll try and tell you the thoughts that came to my mind as I finished telling the story of Masri. Whenever I go to the mosque, I hear the imam say, 'If you could see the future, you would choose the present.' And whenever something happens in the village, people say, 'O Lord, we don't ask you to change your decrees, but please just to soften them a little.' And when disaster strikes, when people die or houses are burnt or crops flooded, they look up at the sky and say, 'Some decrees are less harsh than others.'

Once I used to believe all this. But now, after the disaster that struck me, I have only one thing to say from the bottom of my heart: If I could have foreseen the unknown future, I would never, never have made the choice I did.

4
The Friend

2.30 p.m., Monday, 22 October 1973; 21 Babih 1690 of
the Coptic year; 26 Ramadan 1393 AH

If only I had all the skill of all the story-tellers who've
told their tales since the art began! Then I could do
justice to this difficult task: to set down the part I
played in this strange, sad business. Yet perhaps I
can add a lot that will clarify matters by describing
my side of the events.

I'm writing to you at a critical moment: the afternoon of Monday, 22 October. The date shows he
never had enough time. He was only twenty-four
years old—twenty-four years, four months and nine
days, to be precise. Is that enough? I don't think so.

Why am I starting with all these riddles and puzzles?
I know I'm not making myself very clear, but I do
have an excuse for writing in this mysterious, roundabout way: I'm afraid that if I come to the point right
away, if you realize what I'm going to tell you, you
may not want to go on, for it's a sad, depressing
scene I have to relate, whereas you people in the land
of Egypt are living in times of victory, of happy
laughter and boundless joy. You're a happy people,
happier than our forefathers ever were, and happier

93

than our grandchildren will be. Will you listen to what I'm going to tell you?

Let me set the scene. I'm sitting in the back of a hearse—it's black, but the sun shining on the paint makes it look grey. The plates are the colour of desert sand, with the word 'army' stamped at the bottom. On the platform next to me is a wooden coffin, with Masri's body inside. There's an army driver in the front seat, and a paramedic, and sitting between them a wounded soldier we picked up on the road. The city of Suez is behind us, and we're heading for Cairo. Our job is to hand over Masri's body and bring back a consignment of medicine from the central depot of the Medical Services Division.

I can't take my eyes off the coffin, and I try to stop it sliding around as the vehicle lurches this way and that. Opposite me is a small window, so I can see where we're going and how fast, and I try to make out the road signs so I can figure out when we'll get to Cairo. There's a small radio too, mainly crackling with interference. Every so often, the programme comes in loud and clear, before the vehicle changes direction and the sounds and words fade again.

Masri was wounded in action yesterday and died earlier today, but I still feel as if he's just in a deep sleep, as if he's still alive and there's warmth in his body, seeping out towards me through the cracks in the coffin. The body wasn't stiff when we laid him in the coffin. It was still soft, and it was like blood was flowing in the veins and the heart was beating. He's fainted, I told myself, because of all the trouble he's had lately; soon he'll come round again. His corpse is lying here in front of me, but I still don't believe (I don't think I ever will) that Masri met his death on the battlefield. The fact is, death on the battlefield has a special scent that I've smelled thousands of times lately. Masri's body doesn't have that smell, and I don't believe it ever would, even if I sat here with him like this for months.

Time drags on, slowly and wearily. I think of asking Masri if he really died in action, but the coffin's shut tight. I lean close to it and peer through a crack, but there's no movement inside. Remembering the radio, I fiddle with the knobs, trying to pick up some programme or other. As the vehicle rounds a bend, the newsreader's serious, solemn voice comes in clearly.

'The President of the Republic', he says, 'has announced to the nation that Egypt has accepted the cease-fire recommended by the Security Council yesterday morning. At a meeting held yesterday evening to continue its discussion of the situation in the Middle East, the Security Council gave its approval after an urgent request from the Soviet Union and the United States.'

The vehicle takes another bend, and the newsreader's voice is drowned by the roar of the engine. I look at the wooden coffin, which this time doesn't move in spite of the jolting ride. Perhaps, I think, Masri's listening too, trying to make out what's being said, trying to understand it. Actually, it's not so hard to understand, but everybody has the right to take it in his own way—especially soldiers like us.

Now the coffin shakes again, and it seems to me that Masri understands the riddle, that he's begun to decipher the mysterious clues. The way the coffin's shaking now suggests something more like dissatisfaction, or perhaps an attempt to show disapproval or an effort to explain something when it's a fraction too late.

No doubt this is only the fantasy of a man overcome by weariness and exhaustion before his time. I feel the weariness even now, they say it disappears once you've rested for a while, but I had a break from everything and it hasn't left me; it's just lingered on. I feel weary and dejected, I'm speaking these words almost drunk from exhaustion. The only way out is to talk, like someone moving from one link of a chain to the next without knowing how it's all happening. In the face of the secret I carry with me, everything in my life seems to fade into insignificance; I look in vain for something to compare it with. I doubt whether anything that's ever happened has been like this business of Masri.

I have to concentrate on Masri and what happened to him, because to talk about anything else would be a betrayal of Masri himself. It would be a fatal mistake to treat the various aspects of the story separately, since they're all bound up together. But I'll just talk about Masri, and you can see for yourself how the threads are interwoven and how ridiculous it would be to try and unravel them.

It all started the day I first met him, the day he came to the unit. I'll never forget the first time I heard his voice; it's the first thing that strikes you when you meet somebody, that stream of air from the mouth that's transformed into the voice we hear so clearly. His was diffident, there was something special about it, a desperate appeal for help, for someone to extend a hand and be his friend. When I heard his voice I was aware of that appeal, and when I looked at him I saw his eyes had a look of burning intensity.

If I've neglected the niceties of polite conversation in talking like this—and I suspect I have—my excuse must be that we haven't been formally introduced.

This story doesn't have an author to deal with things like this, so I'll have to do it myself. I'm a friend of Masri's; in fact, circumstances conspired to make me his closest friend. It's circumstances that bring people's destinies together and sometimes twine them round one another, regardless of anything people do themselves; and I now wonder what it was that drew me to Masri like this. How did I get so involved in this sad business? The answer is that I don't know—or at least that there was no obvious reason for it.

But it all goes back to that first meeting, to the way we greeted each other face-to-face one evening. A new batch of conscripts had arrived at the unit, and I was on duty at the company office. It was my job to process them, and I went through the usual questions: name, qualifications, date of enlistment, date of arrival at the unit, place of origin, civilian occupation, intended occupation after discharge, and type of military training received. It was a small batch, eight conscripts from the training camp, and the duty sergeant took them to the barracks, where they stowed their gear and had a bit of a rest—they hadn't been given any assignments, because they'd arrived after ten in the morning, when the day's duty roster is handed out. They asked permission to go out briefly to buy food from the shops around the base, and the sergeant let them go, with orders to return within the hour. They came back punctually.

They were obviously tired after a hard day's travelling—it was one of those tough days for a recruit. The sergeant brought them to me to be registered, and after they'd lined up in front of me, one of them came forward with a stack of papers containing all the necessary information on everyone: rank, name, date of transfer, a statement of the last assignment received from Military HQ before the present transfer, a statement of the last pay received, and information about the sections they'd been attached to. Seven of them had been trained as stretcher-bearers and only one had reached the position of orderly.

He was the one who handed me the group's papers, and I was struck by his modest manner—or what a lifer, a regular army man, would call his slackness and lack of military bearing. He was clearly in charge of the group, though there were no stripes on his sleeve, and yet it was obvious from the way he treated the others that he didn't enjoy the role. I almost told him he didn't deserve to be entrusted with leadership, but somehow the words stuck in my throat; I swear it was his obvious good nature that stopped me. I had another look at him. He was a peasant—it was obvious from his knuckles and his hands—and I could see he was upset. He seemed helpless, yet appealing for help, with some suppressed inner turmoil. It was a brown face, Masri's, the colour of Nile silt.

I started taking down their addresses, and the leader wanted to be put down last—which was strange in itself, since normally a man in his position would put himself before the others. When his turn came, he snapped to attention with military stiffness. I asked his name, because the name on the papers in front of me was so sloppily written I couldn't make it out.

He gave me his first name, but not his father's name or family name, which was what I actually needed. I asked again, and this time he gave his name in full. His details were as follows: came from a village in the Delta, holder of a preparatory school certificate, enlisted at the regional recruiting office in Alexandria, transferred to Military HQ in Hilmiyat al-Zaitoun and assigned to the Medical Services Division, transferred to the basic medical services training programme and then to the training camp, and finally assigned to one of the Cairo military hospitals, where I was serving. He had no address in Cairo, but gave me the name of his village. His occupation before being called up was given as 'student', which made me suspicious. How had a student come to be conscripted? For a moment I thought of asking him why he hadn't used his right of deferment, but I had a lot of work to do. I filled in the rest of the details in the usual way. When I asked him about brothers and sisters, he first said he was an only son with five sisters. I put down my pen and was about to scream at him, telling him he was exempted by law, but before I could open my mouth he slapped his forehead and exclaimed, 'Oh, how could I forget!'

He now said he was the youngest of a large number of brothers, and stammered out an unconvincing explanation for his previous statement. The family was so large, he said, that he'd got mixed up trying to remember the details, especially since this was the first time he'd been asked for all these particulars.

Now I'm a city kid from way back and everything about country life seems a little funny to me. I didn't even know where this peasant conscript's village was; he seemed to come from a world of mystery and myth. Even so, I was struck by the fact that he was a student conscript and couldn't remember how many brothers he had.

He had an explanation for the first point too, saying he was an external student and therefore had no right to defer his military service, but I didn't believe this because he didn't seem convinced of it himself. Obviously something was going on here, and sooner or later it would lead me into his world. I think we both realized he'd have to make a clean breast of it one way or another. 'The heart has its reasons of which reason knows nothing,' and as a human being I've a right to bestow my love on the heart of a friend. I felt this young fellow was tormented by a strong human desire to confess, that he was searching for someone in whom to confide his secret. I'm always prepared to like anyone who lets me read something of what's going on inside him, and from a number of incidents I got the idea that the name he was registered under wasn't his real name, and that there was more to the life than the information given in his papers. There was only one piece of information he knew really well, and that was his date of birth. Every morning at roll call the duty officer would call out the names, checking off any absentees, and we all noticed that he hardly ever answered to the name recorded on our papers. His name would be called out several times, and the officer would be about to mark him absent when one of the soldiers with him would tell him the officer was calling his name. Then he'd answer, and the officer would reprimand him, telling him to wake up and asking sacrcastically if there was anyone else who didn't know his own name.

Or they would tell him to clean his ears out, but exactly the same thing would happen on the following days. I was the only one who really thought about it. I knew he wasn't stupid: on the contrary, he was intelligent and alert, had good hearing and was always quick to respond to situations. After a week of this the commander told him to go for a medical examination, and his hearing was pronounced perfect. The whole thing was soon forgotten, but for me the question marks remained. I had a strong sense that he was living a strange kind of existence: when he took a step in a marching column, it wasn't his step; when he spoke, his tongue was saying words he was forced to say, words that didn't really apply to him. The only things that came essentially from him were a look, a fleeting glance, a sense of excitement, a stirring of the emotions, a certain heartbeat—I don't know how to put all this into words . . .

One evening we were chatting, and he talked a lot about people who go to bed hungry and have barely enough to live on. This surprised me, because, according to the file, his father was an umda, and everyone knows umdas are rich. When I said how astonished I was at his concern for the poor and needy, he blurted out, 'But I'm one of . . . ' He stopped short, and I didn't ask the question that must have been written all over my face. In spite of the mild autumn weather his face was suddenly streaked with sweat, and I didn't want to ask how an umda's son could say he was one of the poor!

Another night we were on duty together. As the man on guard, he had to report to me at 10 p.m. and again at 4 a.m. The first report went as usual, but at the second one he seemed both excited and only half awake at the same time. I took the rifle and the ten rounds of ammunition issued and completed the check, and then, just as he was leaving for the barracks, he said, 'I've realized tonight what my father went through all those years.'

'Your father?'

'He's a night-watchman,' he mumbled in confusion.

THE FRIEND

With a tremendous effort I hid my excitement, pretending nothing was amiss. I realized something strange was going on and wondered what it was all about. The next days were difficult for him, as we talked and talked, always skirting the issue. I felt he was tired of carrying a burden heavy as lead and cold as steel, but I didn't want to press him to tell me what was behind it all. We all have secrets, I told myself, and people have the right to keep them to themselves if they want. I don't remember the exact moment when the torrent of distress building up within him finally burst out.

There were certain standing orders I was officially supposed to carry out with respect to new recruits, although in practice it was never done. It all had to do with metal tags and declarations stating the beneficiary of payments due to someone killed in action and the recognition given to such people. One day we got strict orders to see that metal tags were issued to every member of the force, and to send in copies of the 'declaration in the event of death in action', as it was called, all filled out and certified. When Masri received his metal tag he suddenly stiffened and stared at it there in his hand, asking exactly what it was for. The officer replied that the soldier's name, serial number and blood group were stamped on the tag, and it was hung round his neck by a metal chain. It was a means of identification, since it was the only thing that would stay intact whatever happened to a man on the battlefield, even if his body were burned to a cinder. The tag would establish his identity and testify that it had ringed the neck of a hero.

We gave him the declaration, in which the signatory affirmed, avowed and requested that, in the event of his death in action, all payments should be made to such and such a person. There followed the name of the beneficiary, his relationship to the signatory, his address and the location of the nearest post office where payment could be received. Below the signature was a space for certification by the unit commander, certifying that the signature beneath the declaration was that of the soldier concerned. The document was then stamped and added to the soldier's file. In the event of death in action, it was the only valid authorization for the payment of benefits and for all other matters as well. Everyone remembers Masri's strange refusal to make any declaration. He left the beneficiary's name blank, simply signing the document at the bottom. When the officer asked for an explanation, Masri refused.

'Well, just write the relationship,' suggested the officer. 'Mother or father or sister or something like that.'

He wouldn't even agree to this, but two days later he decided to write just three words: 'the legal heirs'.

That's all he would write on his declaration, and although he was told to be more specific he insisted that what he'd written was enough and the best way out. They all imagined that one of those eternal family quarrels was involved, and assumed that one day he'd come to the office to specify the beneficiary by name.

By the time he handed the declaration to the officer, they'd had just about enough of him. He came to see me at midday, saying he wanted to talk about something important, and we agreed to meet that evening, after the parade to salute the flag and the motherland. But he gave me the slip after the parade, and although I searched for him, I couldn't find him.

By now he'd reached the end of his tether. When

we bumped into each other the following evening, he asked me whether the declaration about death in action had been sent to the military archives yet. I said I didn't know. His second question struck me as strange: did people have the right to change their declaration? I didn't know that either and anyway we saw these declarations as unimportant, strictly routine. My personal opinion, I said, was that changing a declaration would involve revoking it, making out a new one and having the new one certified in the same way as before. It wouldn't be simple.

During the conversation I was concerned with what we were discussing and wasn't paying much attention to him; but while I was running through the complicated measures involved, he was searching for something in his pocket. Apparently he'd hidden it very carefully, since it was inside his armed forces identity card—what he'd done was to split the card in half, put whatever it was between the two parts and then stick them together again, and then put the card back in its protective plastic cover. He took out the piece of paper he'd hidden, folded into a small square the size of the identity card, and smoothed it out carefully. As he opened it, calmly, slowly and carefully, his heart seemed to be beating violently and the expression in his eyes betrayed his emotions. He put it on the table where we sat facing each other, turned it so I could see it, and then took his hand away. I was totally bewildered by this strange turn of events and looked at him quizzically. He glanced at the bit of paper and asked me to read it, saying, however, that he wouldn't answer any questions.

The paper was a copy, not an original, and it had the words 'Ministry of Education' at the top, with

'Cairo Examination Board' directly underneath. The paper certified that the bearer had completed his preparatory education and gave his marks in the various subjects, all indicating a well-above-average performance. In fact his marks were exceptionally high, better than ninety per cent in every subject. He roused me from my thoughts by tapping me on the hand, and when I turned to him he pointed his peasant's finger, without a word, at the name on the certificate. 'Masri,' I read.

Then he pointed at the photograph of the bearer, which clearly corresponded to the person sitting across from me. I hadn't noticed this, I must confess, and didn't know what to make of it at first. I thought there might be two people with similar names or who looked alike, or maybe he had a nickname as well as his legal name. Perhaps, I thought, he wanted to correct the name and have it formally established that the two names belonged to the same person, in which case he would need a paper, signed by two officers and certified by the unit's general staff, to be sent to Military Archives. I was mentally going over the procedures involved—he'd come to me, I supposed, because I work in the administrative office —when he suddenly jerked me out of my thoughts.

'That's me,' he said.

He was pointing at the photograph attached to the certificate, the photograph of a student from the countryside, with a mere wisp of a moustache, a thin beard shaved even before it had sprouted, rather tousled hair and a tie that seemed creased from frequent use—evidently the photographer lent it to every student who came to him for an examination application photograph, and the students wore it for good luck. As for the jacket and shirt, they must once have belonged to a rich student, probably an umda's son, and the photographer lent them to every boy to be photographed in, a kind of uniform.

He moved his finger slowly down the page, pressing so hard I thought he might rub out the writing, and I was afraid he would tear it. His finger came to the student's name, his fingernail next to the initial 'M' of 'Masri'.

'That's my name,' he said slowly, looking up at me.

Well, like I said, I couldn't grasp what it was all about. I was completely nonplussed, and in an attempt to relieve the tension I laughed, raising my hand in the small space across the table between us. We were sitting in a little coffee house in back of the unit.

'What's the story here?' I asked.

He looked into the distance, the early evening street scene reflected in the pupils of his eyes, and began to mumble, 'The story . . . the story . . . the story . . . it's . . . '

It was only, I recall, after he'd repeated the word 'story' four times that all the details came out, and he told me about the day his father had broached the subject with him. He seemed happy as he went over the different parts of the story, as if slaking his thirst at some intoxicating spring. One by one the mysteries written on his face began to melt away and for the first time he came to terms with the things in his memory. Usually he didn't have much to say, but now he seemed drunk with the sound of his own voice, and he relaxed as he talked. He told his story, and as the night wore on I became aware of the mounting excitement within him. The pupils of his eyes dilated and he began to look at life anew. He spoke of how time passed, and how he'd been

unable to finish his studies; how he'd had to leave
them half-way through and endure people's whis-
pered taunts as he walked through the village
byways.

Then he came to the dreadful day his father ap-
proached him. It seemed shocking to me, and all so
utterly bizarre—what Masri told me was the last
thing you'd have expected. This was the first time I'd
pronounced his name, and I found it difficult at first,
because in my own mind the man I was sitting with
still had the name I'd known him by ever since he'd
arrived at the unit. I had a lot of questions when he'd
finished his story, and at first I thought of putting
them off till the next time we talked, but the whole
thing was so painful I finally said to myself, 'Let's
have it all out now.'

I asked the question that was hammering away in
my brain. 'Why did you agree to it?' I asked.

'I had no choice,' he answered quietly.

I wasn't convinced. He hadn't, I imagined, really
accepted that what he'd done was right, and now he
was trying to justify it (more to himself than to me),
still fighting to persuade himself. He launched into a
long speech in which he begged me not to think he'd
been given a lot of money for doing it. He hadn't
even considered the question of payment, he said,
for one simple reason: what he'd done was the only
way out for him and his family.

'I was convinced', he said, 'that we would have to
give our land back to the umda. We went to the
authorities and asked how we could live if he took
our land, and they told us that was beside the point,
we should give up our land first and then we could
go to court about it. The courts were available to
everyone, they said, because this was a time when

justice flourished as it never had in the whole history of Egypt. They said that to trick us, because this was more of a political case than a criminal one. The peasants were divided into two factions over it, with one side maintaining we ought to give up the land and then go to court, and the other swearing they'd never give up the land without bloodshed, even if it meant clashing with the government. Meanwhile the umda was bargaining with a third group, which included my father.

'Then the business about military service came up, and the umda said to my father: "Your son will have to go in return for your keeping the land." My father agreed to this—as a matter of fact the whole family was delighted with the bargain—but I refused to have anything to do with it, I wouldn't even discuss it. Anyway the people in our village don't know what discussion means. The way my family looked at me, I knew they thought I was refusing to do it because I was too selfish to make a sacrifice. They couldn't even see why I should call it a sacrifice. We needed some way out. And then I thought, well, maybe we might find it if I accepted the offer and left the village—who knows?, maybe that's where my future lay anyway. As it happens, I'd already thought of volunteering for military service. I'd even cut out an advertisement, calling for volunteers, from a newspaper one of my friends gave me—it seemed there were a lot of advantages. So I agreed to go, but from that day on I've been in a daze, and I don't even remember how I got to Alexandria. From there I was transferred to Hilmiyat al-Zaitoun and eventually arrived at the unit here.'

Before I carry on with the story, there are a few things that have to be said and set down here, namely, what Masri's thoughts were and how he saw the world. Although he wasn't exactly talkative, what he did say either concerned his determination to get revenge, as he put it, or showed him falling into the depths of despair. 'Masri's lost,' he'd say. No one else ever heard him say that, but I did. No one else will ever feel the burning rage that lay behind the way he uttered each syllable of those words. This obvious passion, which moved me deeply, will remain my own private experience; I can't convey it to you. At the time I imagined I was somehow responsible for what happened to Masri.

Masri was a young man brimming with aspirations, full of the contradictions of our country: love of the world yet indifference to it, daring and shyness at one and the same time, courage and fear, a calm exterior and an inner life seething with rage and rebellion. I have searched long and hard for the right words to describe him, and I think I've finally found them: he was suspicious, sceptical and adolescent, and would have stayed that way if he'd lived to be ninety. When I say 'adolescent', I don't mean that he was always chasing girls; in fact, he never even got to know any in his short life. After he'd told me his tragic story, I wondered whether he might not have been happier if he'd had some experience of that thing called 'love' which people talk about all day long. I don't know.

Masri's adolescent naivety sprang from his suspicion and scepticism; he'd accepted the world unthinkingly, but when he clashed with reality his whole world was filled with uncertainty. Was this why things happened to him as they did? I can't answer that question, for the simple reason that I didn't know Masri before the army. Anything I say should be taken as my own personal opinion, but I think Masri was crossed by fate. Every generation has its destiny; that of our generation of Egyptians, for example, was . . . do I have to go on? Our aspirations were greater than our power to achieve them, and when we took a step forward we found the ground wasn't firm beneath our feet. We looked up at the clouds, but the heavens vanished from above us. At the moment we reached out and grasped the truth about our generation, our leader* sacrificed himself and left us when we needed him most.

I said these last words as the ideas came to me, without really thinking about them; if I'd thought more carefully, I might not have spoken them. I'm talking under stress, because the mere mention of Masri and his story makes me tremble, but I've said words like 'fate' and 'destiny', and that's that. I'm not going to take them back now.

But let's get back to Masri. The chapters of his life were filled with unending agony. Even so, I won't say that what happened was completely due to such things as 'predestined fate' or an 'inevitable destiny', because there was more to it than that. The answer lies in the gulf between the umda's huge white mansion, which gleams even at night, and the house, or rather shack, where Masri's family lived, and in the contrast between the umda himself, with his huge elephant's carcass, and Masri's father, with his skin stretched so tight over his bones they look as if they might pop out at any moment. But I seem to be skirting a question that needs a good deal of thinking about: why did Masri join the army? Was he looking

---

* He is presumably speaking of Gamal Abdul Nasser, who died in 1970 and was succeeded by Sadat.

for a hero's death? He had any number of oppor-
tunities for that, starting with death in defence of his
father's land. I won't raise the issue of the motherland and patriotism, because we all love Egypt in our
own different ways, but which Egypt do we really
love? The Egypt of people dying of hunger or the
Egypt of people dying from overeating? But I've
interrupted what Masri was saying. I said I was
going to explain something, and ended up chatter-
ing. Let me get back to Masri's own account.

'I was called up in place of the umda's son, to protect my family—in fact, it was they who insisted I
should do it. I went, but oddly enough they haven't
been paid yet—we gave in, and that's a road with a
beginning but no end. I went home on leave once,
and told everyone I met that since I'd seen it was
impossible for me to finish my studies, I'd decided to
enlist in the army. That was a realistic, honourable
way out, they said, especially since I could take
classes in the armed forces evening schools; then,
once I'd passed my secondary examinations, I could
go on to university or military college, and when I
graduated there'd be nothing to stop me being pro-
moted higher and higher.

'After I joined the army, the umda—so I learned in
the village—hummed and hawed and didn't give my
father the land. First he took it from him under the
new law and then let him take back part of it under
a share-cropping arrangement. But he categorically
refused to give him any formal contract for this
iniquitous arrangement. I was so angry at the umda's
behaviour that I thought of going to see him, but my
father tried to stop me, saying everything would be
worked out one way or another, and I might compli-
cate things if I interfered. I wasn't convinced, and

decided to see the umda anyway, but he was away—
he was often away at that time! When my leave was
up, I came back to the unit.

'There has to be some way out of this,' Masri said
in a determined tone. I asked him what he had in
mind—was he going to put pressure on the umda to
keep his promise, or what? He rejected that out of
hand; he couldn't face the villagers, he said, because
of the way his father had abandoned the others by
not joining their resistance to the umda. It was true
they hadn't achieved anything—their biggest mistake had been to surrender the land and then go to
court, so that the political dimension of the case was
lost and it became just another court case among
thousands over the last few years. Even though he
was embarrassed about what his father had done,
Masri thought there was no alternative but to reveal
everything.

'But how?' I asked in astonishment.

'I'm going to ask for an interview with the commandant,' he replied quietly, 'and tell him the whole
story.'

'But you were part of the whole crooked scheme,' I
objected, 'and you'll be punished for it.'

'I'll never rest if I don't have it out.'

'But what about your family's future?'

'Have you ever heard of anyone in this country
actually dying of hunger?' he asked sternly. 'We'll
start from scratch, and I'll look after them till the day
I die.'

'Aren't you afraid of the umda and his power in
the village?' I asked.

He hesitated, and then said, 'To hell with fear and
caution!' He suddenly looked very serious. 'From
now on I'll never be afraid of anybody.'

We'd had a long talk, and I felt Masri wanted to apologize for taking up so much time. He looked at his watch—it was just after midnight—and I reminded him that it was Ramadan. I told him I'd rather wait up til the pre-dawn meal than have a nap, which would only spoil my appetite and make it hard to sleep afterwards. He said I was just being polite, so I swore I'd meant to stay up till the pre-dawn meal anyway, whether we had talked or not, because it was an old Ramadan custom for us city people to sit up like that.

I have to admit I was pleased Masri had spoken the way he did, because all my questions had now been answered. I was happy he'd finally decided to open up the whole thing. When he was telling me the story and got to the part where he accepted the umda's offer, I felt I'd lost a man I'd grown to love; but when he said that he'd never be afraid again, I realized I'd found him again. I resolved to stand by him to the end.

He roused me from my daydream. 'Imagine what would happen if I died,' he said. 'Do you realize the position that would put my family in? Who would profit by my death?'

'Stop all this worrying about what might happen later,' I told him. 'Just concentrate on what we're talking about now. Let me help you fix your mind on the truth you've discovered about yourself tonight. I don't know whether to congratulate you or tell you that this discovery means the start of a lot of problems.'

'I'm not worried about the problems,' he replied. 'I'm ready for them.' I should congratulate him, he said, because something momentous had happened that night. He had found himself again, the old Masri who'd been lost, and he had every intention of building on what he'd found.

'Congratulations . . . ,' I replied, laughing.

I wasn't used to calling him by his new name, his real one, and he finished my sentence for me. 'Say it—congratulations, Masri!'

We agreed to set the ball rolling next morning, at the assembly, when he'd ask the commanding officer for an official interview with the commandant, making sure his request was entered in the hospital daybook.

At the assembly Masri raised his hand and said he was requesting an interview with the commandant. When the officer asked him why, he replied that it was a private matter and he couldn't go into it at a public parade. The officer insisted, but Masri refused to say anything more. The officer then promised to enter his request in the daybook, which he would hand to the commandant when he arrived. After the parade Masri was too nervous to do any real work, and I thought of taking him out to a coffee house, but it was Ramadan and we were both fasting. But I did keep him with me till I'd finished some of my work, because I could feel how desperately nervous he was. It was ten o'clock, and there were still two hours to go, since the clerks usually presented their reports to the commandant at noon. After a while we heard that the commandant wasn't with the unit; he'd been called away to an urgent meeting at headquarters. No one knew whether he'd come back to the unit when he'd finished or go straight home.

Masri's forebodings when he heard this were indescribable, and I was surprised at how angry and nervous the news made him. 'One day won't make any difference,' I said. 'There's no need to get so worked up. Today's Wednesday, tomorrow's Thursday, and even if the commandant isn't here by then, Saturday isn't far off.'

Masri thumped the desk with his clenched fist. I tried to calm him down, but it was no use, and by the end of the day I realized that he had a remarkable premonition about what the next day would bring. When the commandant hadn't arrived at noon, I supposed it would all be put off till the following day, but about six o'clock we were met by the unusual sight of almost all the unit's officers arriving with the commandant. Everyone said something really big must be up, with the commandant and all the officers arriving at this hour. There were long meetings between the commandant and his adjutants, the general staff of the hospital, the chief of administrative and technical affairs and the company commander. We soon heard the news: a state of emergency had been declared, all leaves were cancelled, and all future leaves suspended.

The news came as no surprise to some of us, since reserves had been called up the day before. They come here for occasional training, but this time they had all their equipment with them—in fact, this had been going on since the beginning of October—though nobody'd thought anything of it. Then a succession of orders came down: people with certain qualifications were to be transferred to the front immediately.

The commandant ordered the completion of all unfinished business, and Masri was summoned to see him immediately, since no one knew what might happen the next day. He didn't seem particularly worried as he got ready to go to the commandant's office, and he returned in good spirits after a meeting of just a few minutes. He didn't tell me what they had said, but went straight to the barracks to get his things ready. In fact he was in such a hurry that he wouldn't answer any questions, and I had to grab him physically to find out what had happened. 'I'm off to the front,' was all he said.

'What happened?'

'Nothing. Instead of lodging my complaint, I asked for a transfer to the front, in any capacity, as soon as possible.'

'What about all the things we talked about?'

'I was ashamed to talk about a personal problem with Egypt on the verge of a war of liberation.'

'Who told you there's going to be a war?'

'I could feel it.'

'There've been states of emergency before, with no war afterwards.'

'Things are different this time.'

'But what about your real identity, and all the rest?' I cried.

'Problems and legal suits can wait for a few days, or months, or even years,' he said, 'but the liberation of our country can't wait.' 'When we come back,' he went on, 'with the first stage of the war of liberation over, we'll tackle the second stage, which is about solving internal problems. Don't worry, everything will be all right.'

'Did you give the commandant any hint of what you wanted to tell him?' I asked.

'This isn't the time.'

I told him that if he was too embarrassed to talk about it in the present atmosphere, I was ready to speak on his behalf, but he refused. In ordinary circumstances, he said, there were a thousand differences between him and the umda's son, but now it was as if they were the same person, since differences of name, appearance and features didn't mean anything any more. He was determined to share in the honour of liberating Egypt; this was the important thing, not his name or position. He'd told this to the commandant in a different way, and said that going to the front would give him the only satisfaction he sought—the recovery of his lost self-respect.

Masri's words left many questions unanswered. Did he really want to die on the battlefield? In what spirit was he going to the front? Was it a gesture of protest or a willing sacrifice? In a way he'd already been killed in the internal battle before even facing the foreign enemy. The whole thing is so confusing. Talking about it now I feel the blood of a man who was close to me flowing in my veins, and he remains a responsibility I still carry. 'Masri's lost.' He said that several times, and now all I can do for him is weep at his memory and talk about him, and what use is that? When a man dies, he's cut off, and even those who were closest to him carry on their weary path through life. Was it his fault? Or mine? To me his story means only one thing: that there's no justice in this world of ours, and that if we respect our humanity we must demand justice from God—and if He refuses that demand, we'll just have to look for another Lord. Justice means only one thing: that power and strength should be on the side of the powerless individual who is right.

I hope none of you will ask me things like: 'What did you ever do for Masri?' or 'Why are you pinning your hopes on heaven, with all its mists and myths of the unknown?' or 'Where's your faith in man's ability to work out his own destiny?'

Let's get back to Masri and his strange insistence

on going to the front. I tried to talk him out of it, but he just went on with his preparations and paid no attention to me. I'll never understand it: the orders specified certain qualifications, and his weren't among them. All recruits have a special field—a classification, as military jargon has it—and in this case they needed stretcher-bearers, radiologists, lab assistants and people to work in the mobile field kitchens. Masri had been trained as a nurse, and though they hadn't asked for nurses, he insisted on going—I've never in my life met a young man like him. Some of us managed to get out of being sent to the front: if you were, say, related to people in high authority, or related by marriage to high-ranking officers, or if you could get top government officials to ring up and ask that you be granted leave from time to time. The unit's telephones rang constantly, relatives speaking in the soft voices of people who'd never known suffering, asking for the men in question not to be sent to the front. What difference would one soldier make? Besides, these soldiers from good families were special cases: one had a firm that benefited the country, another had a family to support, the father of a third was abroad on an official mission. And so on.

Masri was unique. His way out of his problem, I supposed, was to rush off to the Canal Zone, where he'd be purified in the waters, and the sufferings of so many long years would be washed away.

He came up to me, wanting to talk. He suddenly got excited, full of emotion that hadn't been there before. He told me that the main reason he'd agreed to serve in the army in place of the umda's son, and why he'd refused to say anything about it that day, was that what he was doing wasn't stealing or smuggling, but undertaking a patriotic duty for Egypt. He loved Egypt passionately, and his name, Masri, was the only thing that brought any happiness into his empty life. He didn't know whether he had been given this name accidentally or deliberately, but he loved his father for it, he said, because it had bound his very name to the country he loved so much. This was the only time I ever saw Masri so excited that his face was flushed and covered with beads of sweat.

As he was getting ready to go, a new man was taking shape inside him. Before he left, they reminded him that if he wanted to make any changes in his declaration about death in action, he should put them on record before his transfer, but he replied that he had none. Then he took me aside, telling me that I was the only one who knew his secret and that if he didn't come back I should do what I could to set things straight. He'd been unfairly treated in life, he added, and didn't want injustice to follow him into the other world. Well, I intend to give testimony in this case, and it wouldn't be in anyone's interest to drag in any emotional scenes—I don't want to fill your eyes with hot tears over Masri but to reflect together on what happened. So I won't tell you how I said goodbye to Masri when it was time for him to go, or mention how symbolic it was that he should leave at midnight on a bleak autumn night, or even say anything about the last words spoken on occasions like this.

The following day the unit received orders for more men to be sent to the front, and I asked to go along with the group, because I wanted to join Masri. It was deeply moving when we met again: the young man with all those problems inside had now become a brave combat soldier. He'd only been there for a day when I arrived, but it seemed to me as if he'd been there for years. Taking me by the hand, he showed me all round the camp, and his love for the place convinced me that he regarded it as home. It was obvious, during the few minutes we had together in the midst of the preparations and bustle, that he still wanted to discuss his problem, but circumstances didn't give us a chance.

I arrived at the front at noon on Friday, and the war of liberation began twenty-four hours later, so time was short; but our keenness made it seem an eternity. As soon as our unit got to full strength, we dug trenches, filled huge numbers of sacks with sand and used them as ramparts. We put up tents for administration and sleeping quarters, a tent for use as an examination room and another as an operating theatre; but the largest tent was allocated as quarters for the wounded. Another, they told us, was to be used for autopsies—knowing this, we felt depressed as we levelled the site, drove in the pegs and made the poles fast. Now all that was left was to arrange the camouflage and dig hollows to hide the vehicles. We set up a field kitchen and stashed medical supplies, ammunition, weapons and field rations.

After all this I had administrative duties, getting together a daybook for the orders of the day, a register of the forces assigned to the unit, a daybook for incoming and outgoing messages, and another for the changing of the guard. It was demanding, exhausting work, but we were so happy we weren't conscious of feeling tired, and as the night wore on the duty officer found it difficult to get us to go to sleep.

Our unit wasn't a hospital for treating the wounded

or receiving the bodies of men killed in action. Its functions were clear from its name: Field Sorting Hospital Number One. It was an advance hospital at the front lines, receiving fresh cases and putting them into categories. Some would be given first aid and sent straight back to the battlefield, while others would have a full examination. As for those killed in battle, we'd carry out the normal procedures in such cases.

More than a platoon of nurses and stretcher-bearers were needed at our front line, and we were told to raise the flag of the Medical Services Division, since it was against international agreements for the enemy to fire at us. The commander of the field hospital stood up to assign those who were to go up to the very front line, which at that time, Saturday morning, was the west bank of the Suez Canal. It was seven o'clock, and we were lined up for the morning assembly. Masri was standing on my right, wearing army fatigues which hadn't been pressed, though it was obvious to me he'd put them under his pillow the night before, so they'd look as if they had been. When the commandant announced that he was choosing men for the front line, Masri raised his right hand. He trembled as he resolutely uttered a single word: 'Sir!'

Even before he had been given permission, Masri fell out of line, walked quickly round the row, stood directly before the commandant, and saluted. The officer returned the salute and asked what was up, whereupon Masri replied that he wanted to be the first man into the fighting. This pleased the officer, who saluted him and ordered his name to be put at the head of the list. I wanted to go with him, but the nature of my work wouldn't allow it—I was on the administrative staff, and my natural place was in the unit itself.

Now I have to tell you about the last time I saw him. When the first platoon had been chosen, with Masri put in charge, they went off to be issued bandages, medicine, field rations, gas masks and flasks of water. The issue went quickly, with no hitch. I didn't get a chance to talk to him, but I saw him helping one of his comrades carry a stretcher; he'd fastened the items he'd just been issued to his fatigues. I saw him up on a mound, silhouetted against the endless desert sands. He turned towards us before the platoon moved off, and I was sure that, for all the mild autumn weather, there were beads of sweat on his face; I distinctly remember this because his face seemed to reflect the sun's rays. The platoon moved off slowly eastwards, but Masri was walking so quickly that his body seemed different, the top half leaning forwards; you may say I'm exaggerating, but Masri's body seemed shaped like a bow aiming east. That was the last time I saw him on his feet.

It was two weeks before I saw him again. The platoon was supposed to be relieved at regular intervals because of the tough conditions, and in fact most of the men did come back, but Masri stayed out there. The heroism he showed was indescribable. Talking about it all I can think of are clichés, language seems hackneyed and feeble. It was the evening of Sunday, 21 October, during the last ten days of Ramadan, and the moon came up only late at night. They said that Laylat al-Qadr would be seen during the remaining evenings of Ramadan and that soldiers on night duty should try and catch a glimpse of it. That night, a little before midnight, they brought Masri in on one of his platoon's stretchers. He'd been hit in the neck by shrapnel and wounded in the stomach too, and his left foot was shattered. Even though he was wounded himself, he'd kept working among the other wounded men, not telling anyone he'd been hit. It was only when he fainted that they discovered his multiple injuries. He'd lost a lot of blood, and one of his wounds had become infected.

The moment he arrived, I dropped what I was doing. I saw from the faces of the doctors who examined him that he had no chance, but the commandant ordered that everything possible be done even so. I stayed with him through his feverish delirium, in which he spoke of only one thing, begging me to go and see his family and make sure justice was done. He told me that I knew his story and that he had died in battle as Masri, not as the umda's son. Whatever happened, the truth had to come out. He hadn't been any use to his family while he lived, and he wanted his death in battle to provide them with a safe refuge against an uncertain future.

I agreed to do what he said, but I never thought Masri would really die. If only we could have transferred him to a base hospital, or even a decently equipped district hospital! He was delirious most of the night. I had been ordered to go to Cairo to get some medicine from central stores, and considered getting excused so I could stay with Masri, but I was embarrassed to ask. We looked for a small lorry, and it turned out the most suitable means of transport was the hearse: its large rear section could be locked, which made it ideal for transporting medical supplies.

As we were making arrangements for the work order and papers to present to the military police, the field telephone to regional headquarters rang. The message was to order a cease-fire as of 6:45 that evening. Before this bitter news could sink in, they told me that Masri was dying. I raced to the tent, and found he was going fast. It was all over in minutes. I stretched out his legs, then placed his hands next to his body and closed his eyes. When we told the unit commander, he asked us to take the body with us to Cairo, and then on to his village for burial. The body was quickly prepared and a death-in-action certificate filled out.

So there I was, sitting in the back of the vehicle. The radio was still on, but I'd changed the frequency. A solemn voice was saying, 'At 6:45 this morning Field Marshal Ahmad Ismail Ali, minister of war and commander-in-chief of the armed forces, issued orders to all armed forces' formations for a cease-fire to begin at 6:45 p.m., Cairo time, 22 October 1973, if the enemy ceases fire at the time agreed.'

We reached Cairo that evening, and from the window I could see life going on just as when I'd left seventeen days before. I saw a young girl carrying fresh loaves of bread, blowing on her fingers because the bread was so hot. In one of the dark, empty streets, I saw a young man and a girl holding hands, secret messages passing between their eyes, and an old woman begging for alms from the early evening loiterers.

We went to the hospital. It was a long way away from the central square of a hushed city that had settled down for the long night ahead, yet it was pervaded with the silent smell of war. I went into the hospital through the rear door used for stretcher cases, and we carried Masri to the autopsy room and opened the coffin. We were groping in the darkness because of the black-out, and I couldn't make out Masri's features. I wanted to strike a match to get a last glimpse of that tired, strained face, but the black-out was still in force and, having just come from the front, I knew as well as anyone how serious it was. The soldier on duty in the autopsy room went out and bought two slabs of ice, which we broke into small pieces and packed around the corpse.

I asked about the consignment of medicine I'd come for, and was told the depot had sent it that morning and I'd have to wait three days for another consignment. So as it turned out I would be able to accompany my dear friend to his village. The officer will tell you about that journey, and about what happened when we got there—I've said enough. I'm not the sort of Cairene who's never been out of the city and is proud of it. No, it wasn't the first time I'd been to the countryside. But it was the first time I'd had a really good look at it.

So let me add a word about what I saw there. Some of you, I know, may be asking what all this has to do with the war that took place in the land of Egypt and the novels and stories written about it (the tales of the war will be a best-seller for all those story-tellers and novelists who like to flirt with the authorities and powers-that-be—until the next war comes along). But I want to tell you about my trip.

I don't know why, but I was anxious to see Masri's family most of all, his father, mother and sisters. I felt I knew them already, because Masri had told me all about them when we'd talked together, but it was the first time I'd met Masri's father in the flesh. I felt I'd made his acquaintance twice: once in what Masri said about him, and now this second time. He had an open face, which reflected every emotion as it came. I don't know why I felt attracted to his mother, but from the moment I first set eyes on her one word stuck in my mind and came to my lips without thinking: *'Fellaha!'*, peasant woman.

I tried to remember all I'd been told about her. As I spoke, I wanted desperately to make her feel the human bond that had existed between me and her only son. When she replied her words were mingled with tears; every word drew a tear from her eyes and tore a sob from her desolate heart. Ashamed of weeping in front of a stranger, she tried to hold back her tears, so it sounded like the cooing of doves in a dovecote. She tried to smile, and swallowed her tears, and then her face was distorted by a grimace which could not conceal her distress.

On the way back I felt like crying because, after certain developments you'll hear about later, Masri's family wanted to show their love for me in every possible way. I gave it all a great deal of thought, but do I have the right to express my thoughts here? Well, I'm asking you to let me do just that. I was sitting outside the umda's dawar, and the dark night was filled with all the mysterious sounds of the country. It seemed like a secret code. The investigation was going on inside, and as I sat there my thoughts ebbed and flowed like the waves of the sea. I'd seen endless pain and misery on my way to the village, and prayed to God to have mercy on our country and deliver it from its suffering. When, I wondered, would God release Egypt from this torment and misery and grief? No one knows the answer, but things surely can't go on as they are much longer.

Where was divine justice in Masri's story? If there were any justice, God would grant the poor the rights they're trying to uphold. They've got right on their side, but since when has right mattered against power? Right on its own is helpless—it's a rifle that fires back into the breast of the person holding it, it's a broken wooden sword. Masri's family own nothing but their bare hands, while the umda is powerful and never tires of repeating that his power comes from God—which is apparently true! The simple truth is that if God has chosen to be Lord of the rich alone, then the poor's only recourse is to look for a Lord of their own. Maybe they'll find one, who knows? Perhaps he's been waiting for them ever since the world came to know of the vast, ever-widening gulf that separates the poor from the rich.

Here we are, I thought, returning from the battlefield only to find that the times of blood in our country have already begun. Have we come back from one war only to find there's another one waiting for us? I think it was our mistake, because in the war they halted only yesterday there was an enemy behind us too. Every bullet fired towards occupied Sinai should have been matched by another one fired back towards enslaved Egypt, which has occupiers of a different sort—poverty, backwardness, injustice and oppression. But we didn't realize this. We directed all our efforts against an enemy that was plainly visible, and neglected the malignant, cancerous enemies that can't be seen with the naked eye. We had an excuse. We thought the people at home would take up this task in our place, but they failed to live up to our expectations—which means that we ourselves must now undertake it. It won't wait—otherwise the cancer will spread through the body of the nation, making the cure more difficult. Who knows?, the disease might spread so rapidly that the only possible treatment would be extermination of the whole body. The better of the two solutions is still a painful one.

The lesson I learned so clearly is that our country is like a cat that mercilessly eats its own young. These children go out into the world like fish, the big fishes devouring the small. Take a close look at the present situation in our country—it's a strange world that is sown with mines yet imagines it's safe; it's both prickly and easy-going, loving and malicious, sated and starving. In any case, it's ours, and there's the rub—does this country really belong to us, and since when, and to which of us exactly? Don't you agree that the expression 'It's our country' has a lot of different meanings?

I wished (what can we do but wish these days!) that the war was still on, so that I could shed a drop of my own blood, the last blood to be shed in defence of the land of the Nile Valley, and so conclude my chapter of this story. But the time of wars is over in Egypt, and the time of talk has begun; and words set one another ablaze, and the land of Egypt will never know anything but words.

I wished . . . but let's forget about all that. Right now I've got just one task: to keep quiet. Silence speaks louder than talk at a time when everyone's swimming in a sea of words.

5
The Officer

I thanked God I hadn't known him; I'd never so much as laid eyes on him. It was the day before yesterday when I arrived at the unit and presented my papers to the commandant, and only one day later I was given this assignment; everyone else, apparently, had avoided it because of its depressing nature. I thought of protesting but I didn't want to start off by making excuses and refusing an assignment, especially since my unit commander, when I'd presented my papers to him, had concentrated on one particular point: 'Are you an officer on active duty or a reservist?'

'A reservist, sir,' I replied, in a normal voice.

He didn't look happy, in fact he looked distinctly worried. I'd been told that taking the bodies of men killed in action back to their home towns to hand them over to their families was the very essence of my job as a social services officer. There were three of us in the unit's social services, the other two being a young girl with the rank of first lieutenant and a woman with the rank of major. It wasn't reasonable to expect either of them to take on this job.

I received my instructions and left. From the day I'd arrived, the autopsy room had been the one thing

I found upsetting. On the two previous days it had been surrounded by crowds of people coming to collect bodies—this being, apparently, a daily occurrence. But this time when I got there I didn't see anyone, which surprised me, but when I read the dead man's address I understood why—he wasn't from Cairo. I went to the company commandant, who was an honorary officer with the rank of captain. After I introduced myself we shook hands, and I asked him to designate the men who'd go with me on this assignment. He pressed a button and told the orderly to fetch the head of the company office, so he could select the men in question. The soldier dealing with the addresses of members of the force came over from the regimental office, as instructed, bringing two copies of the official address of the deceased. He gave me the original and I signed his copy, asking if he happened to know the way to the village.

'No,' he replied shortly.

'You can't get lost if you ask the way,' I remarked, to reassure myself.

The soldier went off and came back with the head of the company office. They both asked if I'd mind a soldier friend of the deceased going with me; he'd been the dead man's closest friend and he thought he knew the way to the village.

'Is there any reason why he shouldn't go?' I asked.

'On the contrary, he wants to go with you.'

At this point a soldier in fatigues came in, saluted me and the commanding officer and said he had urgent reasons for requesting permission to go to the deceased's village.

'Are you from the same village?'

'No.'

'Then why are you so keen on going?'

'Special circumstances.'

The commanding officer gave him to understand that there was no objection, but the problem was that he didn't belong to our unit; since his transfer to the field, he'd been regarded as attached to Field Sorting Hospital Number One, the only quarter that could grant or withhold permission for him to go on an official assignment. Besides, he'd come to our unit in another capacity, to collect a consignment of medicine from the central depot. Could this wait till he came back?

According to the soldier, the medicine wouldn't be delivered for another three days. He then asked why he shouldn't go in an unofficial capacity, and the officer agreed. I was afraid there wouldn't be enough room for him in the vehicle, and I also wondered about possible objections and harassment by the military police, but since he was the only person who'd known the deceased, and probably the only one who knew his family and the way to the village as well, it would be better to have him with us than to rush off alone and get lost in the countryside, especially as we'd get to the village at night. This was my first assignment, and I was anxious to see it brought off successfully. Another soldier was also assigned, together with an NCO, a driver and a civilian mechanic in case the vehicle broke down on the way. I secured an order from the company office that they should come with me on the assignment, and the pass was issued.

I left the company office together with the deceased's friend. He was clearly upset, but I didn't think anything of it, putting it down to grief over his comrade's death. He'd probably seen the man killed at the front before his very eyes—a thoroughly distressing experience for anyone. As we sat waiting for some papers to arrive, his face registered other emotions besides grief, and I wondered whether it was anxiety, awe in the face of death, or sorrow. His right hand shook, and I distinctly remember he wanted to tell me something, but couldn't decide whether to or not; perhaps I didn't give him sufficient encouragement, though I'm a friendly, sociable sort of person and it only takes a moment for me to get to know people. When he said nothing, I thought he must be intimidated because I was a new officer, which was stupid of me. Agitation and emotion showed on his face, and he was wringing his hands so hard he almost cut off the circulation. Nervously he struck his head with his hand.

'Is something wrong, private?' I asked.

He opened his mouth and seemed about to speak, but the words died on his lips. Nothing came out, and, as for me, I had no time to stand and wait. I went out, leaving him with a burden and a secret that would inevitably have to come out. After I'd reached the village and heard the whole story, I was sorry I hadn't listened to him—I could have helped him and been a friend to him. But would that have changed anything or prevented what happened? I don't think so, because it was too serious, its implications too great. I called the corporal, who was the leader of the group going with me, and told him to be sure to bring the deceased's belongings.

'And don't forget the photos of Masri when he was in the unit,' his friend added.

'Who's Masri?' I asked him.

'The deceased,' he replied.

I supposed that 'Masri' must be his nickname and that the name on my papers was his real name.

'Masri'. Was that his nickname?' I asked.

'Do the poor have nicknames?' he answered, and went on to explain: 'The name on your papers is the right one—I wasn't using "Masri" literally. Doesn't the name "Masri" belong to everyone in this country?'

He seemed normal enough, but when, on our way to the village, he warned me not to mention the name 'Masri', I realized something was wrong, something I didn't know about, but I didn't think any more about it at the time.

When I went up to the office, I asked the woman in charge of the department about the rest of the procedure. I inquired whether she had any fixed printed instructions she could give me, or a manual, so that I could carry out the formalities properly. She replied, with a smile, that there were no manuals or written instructions; they'd learned the proper procedures in circumstances like this from the people who'd done the work before them.

She brought a pen and paper and asked me to note down the various steps. I told her I had a good memory and wouldn't forget anything.

'Everybody says that,' she remarked, in the tone of someone who knows what she's talking about, 'but they forget a lot when they're actually doing the job.' Obediently I started to write.

'In the event of the death in action of a member of the armed forces,' I wrote, 'whether from the ranks or non-commissioned officers, the following ten-point procedure should be observed with respect to their burial' (I learned later that there were special procedures for officers, quite different from those followed for NCOS and privates):

'1. Confirmation that there is a certificate or

statement of death in action on the form prepared for that purpose by the Printing and Publications Department of the Armed Forces; and that the form has been properly filled out, signed by two eye-witnesses and countersigned by the chief-of-staff and the unit commander. The form should give particulars regarding the day, hour and place of death and a summary of the circumstances.

'2. If, because of the circumstances of the operations, there is no certificate, a committee of investigation shall be set up under the supervision of the monthly review board to confirm death in action and to provide the foregoing information in full.

'3. The procurement of an official document giving the deceased's address, since knowledge of the address is the only means of reaching the deceased's family promptly. The address should be confirmed by a responsible officer, or at least adjutant, and should be taken from the latest register of addresses, preferably the register instituted in connection with current operations, since it is usually the most accurate.

'4. A request for a copy of the combatant's declaration recorded in his own handwriting, stating his beneficiary in the event of his death. If more than one declaration is found in his file, the most recent will be followed.

'5. The surrender to the beneficiary of the articles found on the body of the soldier after his death in action. The articles will have been noted in an official report, and the signature of the beneficiary on this report will be sufficient.

'6. The payment of funeral costs and granting of immediate financial aid to the family by the Personnel

Department, estimated in accordance with standing instructions regarding non-commissioned officers and men of the ranks.

'7. The procurement of a death certificate and a permit for the burial of the deceased from the health office nearest his unit, on the basis of the unit's report of his death in action.

'8. Confirmation of his preparation for burial in the unit's autopsy room; of his being placed in a shroud there; and of his being placed in a well-sealed coffin before transport to his home town.

'9. Upon arrival in the home town, the officer will report the matter to the local authorities and then proceed at once to the village graveyard. He will then ascertain the identity of the deceased's relatives and take them to the graveyard in the presence of the local authorities. There the deceased will be taken directly from the army vehicle to the grave without the coffin being opened by anyone.

'10. After returning from the assignment, the social services officer will write a detailed report of the steps he has taken, and also (since he has the right to suggest amendments to the procedure), set down his recommendations and suggestions.'

I took the sheets on which I'd written down the ten steps and studied them carefully. Then I made out my plan of action. Calling the NCO who was to go with me, I told him to take responsibility for obtaining the burial permit and death certificate, for securing a copy of the deceased's stamped and accredited declaration regarding his beneficiary and for seeing to the preparations for his burial (incidentally, the bodies of men killed in action mustn't be washed). I myself went to the Personnel Office to see to the financial side, and instructed another soldier to obtain a road permit for the vehicle and a written order for the petrol tank and reserve tank to be filled. I arranged to meet them in two hours at the autopsy room.

Going out into the bustling streets, full of young men and women, and thousands of people going about their daily business, I was struck by the wide gulf that separated us from them. Then I remembered I'd arranged to meet some friends after the *iftar** to tell them about my first day as an officer, and I realized that now I wouldn't be able to meet them unless by some miracle, I got back from my trip before the iftar. I didn't think I'd make it, so I decided to get in touch with one of the group and apologize for not meeting them as agreed, telling them I had to go on an assignment whose nature I couldn't discuss over the telephone and couldn't disclose till I returned, especially in view of the critical state the country was in. It was only an ordinary job, but there was no harm in pretending it was something special.

We were to have met in a furnished apartment in Aguza—a middle-class area of Cairo—which I'd rented along with three of my mates. One of our group was in the army like me, another had been exempted because he was the only son in a family of girls and the fourth had evaded the call-up by methods I prefer not to mention. The apartment didn't have a phone, and each person did as he liked in the place, the only rule being that he had to tell the others in advance when he was going to be in, so no one would intrude. I decided I'd get in touch with

*Iftar: the meal eaten after sundown, breaking the daylong fast during Ramadan.

136

one of them when I came back. I thought of going home to get a few things—a change of underwear, pyjamas, an electric razor and a towel—but then thought better of it, because everyone had said that the procedure in the deceased's village wouldn't take longer than an hour and might be over in a matter of minutes. The dead man's family would associate me with the sad return of their son in a sealed coffin, so no one would try and detain me when I said I was leaving.

I remembered my girlfriend, with her smooth, fair skin, and thought of the wonderful evening I'd intended to spend with her in the Aguza apartment, after getting permission from the others in the group. My friends would have winked knowingly at me and wished me a great evening. I was close to getting really annoyed and exasperated; there was no way to get in touch with her, and my not turning up would mean long months of quarrels and reproaches, with me offering excuses and explanations.

In the offices I found civilian employees and officers in luxurious surroundings. The carpets beneath their feet were so thick that your shoes sank right into them; the heaters by their desks glowed red (even though winter hadn't arrived yet); and they had telephones to hand which would suddenly ring to bring them word of how someone was, or give them the price of meat, or promises of help in getting hold of supplies of chickens, or the latest black-market rate for the dollar, or the best place to have a good night out. I handed over the papers I was carrying, certifying that, two days earlier, one of Egypt's sons had died for her in action. I expected them to show some respect when looking at the papers and, since my assignment was very meaningful, to give me all possible assistance in carrying it out. So I was taken aback when a man sitting behind an iron grille looked angrily at the papers, then at his watch, and snapped, 'You should have got here earlier, mate!'

I studied his face as he examined the papers. I couldn't detect any change in him. He gave them back to me, saying, 'The stamp on the death-in-action certificate isn't clear; it'll have to be stamped again.'

I told him that the unit was at the front line.

'So what?' he replied.

I explained that the deceased had been dead for three days now. He motioned me to keep quiet and pointed to a small door on his right, asking me to take it up with the boss. The boss was sitting with a long string of prayer beads in his hand, muttering to himself in a low voice. I spoke, but he didn't reply till he'd finished the words he was repeating. His fingers still played with the beads in his right hand as he held out his left to take the papers. He looked at them for a long time. His lips were moving again, and I hoped this meant he was reading what he had in front of him. Having learned the reason for the first man's objection, he declared that he'd acted correctly and was only carrying out the standing orders he'd been given. Our discussion was irritating and quite unnecessary. Finally, since the situation was so delicate and we'd spent such a long time discussing it, he offered me a way out. I should make out a statement, he said, that the stamp on the certificate was genuine, giving full particulars about myself and assuming total responsibility if the stamp turned out to be false.

I went back to the hospital feeling worn out, and

sat down to wait for the people who'd gone to fetch the various papers we needed. Then I managed to get in touch with one of my friends to say I wouldn't be able to meet them as arranged. Finally we all assembled and put the coffin containing the body in the back of the vehicle. The mechanic, the deceased's friend and one of the two men detailed to go with me sat next to the coffin, while the other sat between me and the driver. It was now late afternoon. Before leaving Cairo we worked out how long the journey would take, and found that we'd arrive after the time for breaking the fast. We'd have to break our fast on the way, at Tanta, and then move on to the village; we'd reach it at a convenient time, after the iftar.

I felt in my pocket to make sure I had the slip of paper with the address. It was going to be a long ride. The vehicle was uncomfortable, and the still autumn air was oppressive. We were travelling west on the Cairo-Alexandria Delta highway, with the soft, pale yellow sun in our faces. The hearse was slow, but the driver spoke in its defence, claiming that it was a superior vehicle that could leave anything else behind; he pointed to the speedometer, which went up to 160 kilometres. But to avoid accidents—especially as all the vehicle's journeys would be on highways—the commander of the military expedition had had its maximum speed reduced to only 60 kilometres an hour.

I dozed off with the swaying of the vehicle, leaning my head against the window. The fellow sitting next to me must have dropped off too, as the driver woke us both up and gave us a long lecture on the proper thing to do when sitting next to someone who was driving on the highway. It was because the people sitting next to the driver fell asleep, he said, that there were so many accidents; he made a lot of trips, and relied on conversation with the people sitting next to him; he always stayed wide awake if the passenger was a really good, stimulating talker. The most interesting conversations, he added, were stories, anecdotes and legends. Any mention of science and politics sent him right off to sleep.

'What if you don't find a passenger who's a good talker?' I asked.

He laughed and slowed down. Then he took off his fatigue cap, hung it on the gear shift and started talking. He'd been taught to drive, he told us, by someone who'd learned in the British camps a long time ago; and this man had taught him that, if he happened to be travelling alone and was falling asleep because of the movement of the vehicle, there were steps to follow and memorize like the entries in a multiplication table. The first was to talk to yourself, telling stories your old grandmother had told you on long winter evenings. But stories wouldn't always do the trick, so, when he found his attention straying, he'd come to the second step, which was whistling various simple, well-known tunes and singing loudly enough to wake himself up.

I got bored, even though what he was saying was new to me. 'What would you do', I asked him, to bring his chatter to an end, 'if all this still wasn't enough to keep you awake?'

That was a good question, he replied; it showed an intelligence he'd rarely found in an officer. 'If I don't manage to stay awake,' he said, 'there's still one last way. Do you know what it is?'

Of course not!' I answered, surprised.

Then he'd tell me, he said, expecting his reward

from God alone. This last step was to pull your hair, holding the steering-wheel with one hand, according to whether you were right- or left-handed, and pulling your forelock with the other.

He was stopped from talking by a knocking sound from the rear of the vehicle, meaning that they wanted us to stop. When we got out, we found the men in the back covered in sweat, their faces flushed. They'd nearly chocked to death, they told us, and the smell of the body in the coffin had made the air so foul that one of them had vomited. I realized how difficult it must be to sit with a body that had lain for three days first in a field autopsy tent and then in a hospital autopsy room that lacked decent equipment (even though, so I'd been told that day by the soldier in charge, it had dealt with the bodies from the four wars Egypt had fought).

We took a rest, sitting in the open air while the driver changed the water in the radiator. For the rest of the trip there wasn't a moment's silence. It was the driver who did the talking, this time telling us about all the journeys he'd made with the bodies of people who'd been killed in action or died from ordinary diseases in hospital. His talk, it must be said, turned into a sort of bragging. What singled him out from other people, he told us, was his iron nerves, and to prove his point he claimed that the last driver of the vehicle had gone mad because he'd made so many trips with dead bodies; he was now locked up in a mental hospital. His illness had started with a nervous breakdown, the result of witnessing the moments when the family learned that the person had died, and from seeing the way they acted at the burial. But he'd now done three years in this unpleasant job, and he was still sane.

The last thing he talked about was the person whose body we were carrying today, telling us what he knew of him and calling down God's mercy on him. He asked me whether the dead man was from a village, a district town or a provincial capital and when I said he was from a village, he remarked that village people were generous and brave, though they went too far in their grief.

It was getting near sunset, and we knew the time for breaking the fast had come because there was less traffic and a sudden calm had descended. So we made for the first town on our route to break our own fast, and since I wasn't keen on eating in a restaurant, two of the soldiers went to buy some food from the market. I refused to go to a coffee house, so we sat in the vehicle, eating hurriedly and drinking tea they'd brought from a place nearby. The soldier and mechanic asked permission to go to a local coffee house and smoke a water-pipe, and I told them to make it quick.

Then, when night had fallen outside the town, we set out for the village. The deceased's friend tried to remember the route we had to take, but I was afraid we'd lose our way. We came to the point where we had to leave the highway and turn down a dirt side-road. The way was engraved on the memory of the deceased's friend, so it was easy to pick out the landmarks he gave me. He told me we'd find an overhead bridge by the side of a primary school, next to the railway station. Behind the school were the homes of the railway workers, and opposite these was a level crossing you went over to get to the dirt road.

When we started along this road, we found ourselves in pitch darkness. We stopped, and the deceased's friend got out and made for the crossing, where there was a pinpoint of light from a small fire over which the crossing attendant was making tea. The deceased's friend asked about the village, but instead of answering, the attendant pointed to a peasant sitting next to him. 'You're in luck,' he said to the peasant, and told the deceased's friend that we must be doing a good deed at this blessed time, because the man sitting next to him was going to the same village and was waiting for some kind of transport. He'd ride along with us and show us the way.

The peasant got up and brushed the dust from his gallabiyya—he'd been sitting on the bare ground. The attendant grasped his hand and offered us some tea (we could hear it making a faint, bubbling sound), but we declined with thanks. The peasant got in with us, thanking us profusely and saying that heaven had sent us to him just then; he would have had to spend the night at the crossing, he said, if no car had come along—and, of course, none usually did come before morning.

'Is it far?' I asked.

'No, not very,' he said.

'How many kilometres?'

His answer took a different form. 'Two hours on foot,' he said, 'and a quarter of an hour by car.'

The driver chipped in. In that case, he said, he could assure us from his wide experience that it would be at least ten kilometres. I asked the peasant why he didn't walk it, especially as the climate was healthy here, and the air was pure. He laughed. I obviously wasn't from the country, he said, but from the city, which swam in a sea of coloured lights from sunset to sunrise and was full of policemen armed to the teeth, guarding people and their houses and shops. Here, on the other hand, 'the wolves had been let loose on the dogs'.

I didn't understand, and the fellow went on to tell me that as far back as he could remember, they'd all lived lives of quiet, peace and harmony. But recently, however, gangs had started to appear at night to kidnap, murder and rob; the number of incidents was rising, and no one knew what the future held. Who would have imagined, he asked, that this would happen in the peaceful countryside, with its spirit of generosity, tolerance and harmony? He seemed good-hearted enough, and I liked him—yet all our subsequent troubles came because of him. When he'd finished his stories about the gangs, we all fell silent, a silence broken only by the noise of the vehicle as it moved slowly along the unpaved road. Suddenly the peasant turned to me. 'Who are you going to see in the village?' he asked.

I mentioned the name of the deceased's father as set down in my papers. I remembered it clearly, because of the number of times I'd taken the sheet out to read it.

'He's the village umda,' remarked the man, 'and he's there at the moment.'

The driver, determined to join in every conversation, pointed to the rear of the vehicle and said to the peasant, 'It's sad to be carrying a martyr.'

The man struck his chest in alarm. 'The Lord save us from harm! Who is it?'

'The umda's son.'

'But none of the umda's sons is in the city for medical treatment. Or was it an accident?'

'What do you mean accident?' cried the driver angrily. 'He died on the battlefield!'

'In the war?' asked the peasant.

'Ah! He's caught on at last!'

The fellow thought for a moment, an intent look on his face. Suddenly he raised his hand. 'But none of the umda's sons is in the army!' he said.

'Who told you that?' asked the deceased's friend, speaking for the first time.

'I'm sure of it.'

'We're sure of it too.'

The sudden moment of silence did nothing to reassure any of us. The peasant, who seemed upset and couldn't sit still, was thinking out loud. 'All the umda's sons were exempted from military service,' he said, 'and anyway they're too old now. The only one who should have gone into the army is the youngest, and he's there in the village.'

'When was the last time you saw him?'

'This morning. I said hello to him.'

'Maybe the umda's got a son you don't know about,' said the deceased's friend bitterly.

The peasant sensed the note of sarcasm that had crept into the conversation, and replied even more sardonically, 'Who knows? Maybe the umda's son's got magic powers and can be in two places at once. Aren't we living in an age of miracles?'

And so I found myself caught up in a strange problem. When the peasant started rambling on, I thought it was just empty talk which would make the journey go faster. I didn't realize that what he said was going to bring us up against a problem—one I hadn't anticipated and didn't know how to handle. If I failed in this first assignment, it would affect my future in the unit. To still my rising anxiety, I mentioned the name of the deceased.

For the first time the peasant got angry. 'That sissy!' he shouted. 'He's the umda's youngest son,' he continued, 'and he's a sissy, as anyone in the village could tell you.'

'Is he the person you met today?'

'Yes, that's him.' Thoroughly confused, he then asked, 'But how could he die in action when he was in the village?'

'Perhaps he died in battle by proxy,' suggested the deceased's friend slowly.

The peasant didn't understand this, or the friend's final words: 'By the power of attorney which Egypt gave him to do it.'

I ordered the driver to stop and told him to leave the lights on, then got out and took the peasant with me. I took out the papers and went over the information about the man who'd died in action: name, the name of his village and his father's occupation. All the details were correct, the man said—except that the young man it said had died in action was there in the village. We climbed back in and the driver moved on again, in a brooding silence of anxiety and foreboding. He assured us the story wasn't new to him; he'd seen it happen before, he said. I shouted at him, and he trailed off without finishing what he was going to say. I told him to drive faster, and for the last time asked the peasant if he was sure of what he'd said.

He answered that if we'd only be patient he'd bring the deceased to me himself, alive and well. I asked the deceased's friend if the information we had was correct, and he replied ambiguously, 'We'll see when we get to the village.'

My nerves got the better of me. I'd asked in the unit about every situation likely to arise, and about the measures to be taken in each case; but it had never occurred to me that I might be sent on an assignment only to find that the body I was taking was still alive. I ordered the driver to stop again, got out and opened the back of the vehicle. The corporal was surprised when I asked him to rock the coffin, so I told him I wanted to be sure the deceased was actually in there. After rocking the coffin—with some difficulty—and putting his face close to one of the holes, he assured me the body was still inside, inquiring irritably whether there was really any chance of the body being stolen. Not feeling like talking, I told him to hand over the deceased's belongings. I looked through them and took out the civilian identity card, then called the peasant over and showed it to him by the light of the vehicle's headlights. He held the card so close to his eyes I was afraid he'd hurt himself; I thought he was going to stick the card to his eyelids.

'This is a photo of Masri', he said uneasily, 'the son of the umda's night-watchman.'

The man couldn't read, so I read all the details to him. The name on the card was the umda's son's.

The peasant summed it all up: 'The name belongs to the umda's son, but it's a photo of the night-watchman's son.'

I was completely baffled. I thought of going back to the unit, but the smell of the body made that impracticable; and when the peasant pointed to the lights of the village, saying we'd almost arrived, I decided on a plan of action.

We drove on into the village and stopped in front of the umda's dawar; then we all piled out and went to sit in a small room with a telephone and some rifles in it. I was told that the umda and his elder sons were at their prayers. The peasant disappeared, then came back and assured me in a whisper that the umda's youngest son was in the house. I asked to see him, and a pampered-looking young man appeared. I asked him his name and other particulars, and his answers agreed with the information I had with me, but when I asked him to show me his identity card he replied that his father had kept it, night and day, for the past three months or so, and had refused to give it to him, he didn't know why. As for his status as regarded military service, he assured me that all he knew was that it had been postponed till he finished his studies. When I asked him where the deferment certificate was, he answered that it was at school; and when I asked who'd given it over to the school, he said his father had.

'Did you see the deferment certificate yourself?' asked the deceased's friend.

'No, but I heard about it. Anyway, there must be one, because I didn't go into the army.'

At this point the umda arrived and greeted us, followed by his sons and several watchmen. I took out the papers and started to speak, amazed that he wasn't taken aback by the news. All he wanted was for me to give him the papers, the deceased's belongings and the body, and leave at once with my men. I controlled myself. 'Was the deceased really your son?' I enquired.

He didn't answer straightaway, and the deceased's friend quickly led me out to the vehicle and told me the whole story.

'Did you know all this before we left?' I asked him.

'Even before he died in action,' he answered.

I grabbed him and very nearly hit him, but finally restrained myself. A question I couldn't answer had sprung to mind: why hadn't the deceased's friend alerted me to this complicated business before we set out from Cairo? Had he failed to do so deliberately, thinking he was doing the deceased and his family a favour by letting things happen like this? Perhaps he'd acted out of loyalty. That would explain why he'd insisted on coming with us, even though most people shrink from assignments like this.

The deceased's friend calmed me down. The important thing now, he said, was to deal with this unusual situation, and he warned me about the power and tranny of the umda. I realized I had to avoid making things worse; the umda was on guard now, like a man getting ready for battle. The situation changed, however, when a gaunt-faced peasant came in with a rifle on his shoulder, weeping and shouting. 'I'm the martyr's father,' he said, coming up to us.

The umda's reaction was not so much a retreat as a collapse. It all happened in front of a large number of villagers—virtually the entire populace had gathered outside the dawar by now. The umda tried to get me to go into his house, but I refused; then he demanded that I order the vehicle to move on to the cemetery at once, and again I refused. He told me I'd be responsible if a mob gathered. The village was full of gangs, he said; there were old scores to be settled, and Egypt was going through troubled times. He wouldn't be held responsible for the consequences of the present dangerous situation.

I nearly gave him the body and the papers and the deceased's belongings so I could get back to Cairo, although at the same time I was trembling and upset; but Masri's friend intervened, begging me to go to the district police station. At this, the umda flew into a rage. He was the government's representative in the village, he said, and if there was any problem he

149

would deal with it. We had no legal right to go to the police, unless we were referred by him, as long as we were in the village he administered.

I had three alternatives. One was to go to the district police station whose jurisdiction the village came under and take the necessary action. But there was also a military aspect to my problem: and our instructions were that we should look for the nearest military police post, which would then take charge of the matter—but how could I look for such a post at night, with everything pitch-black? My third altern-ative was to go back to Cairo, where the commandant would take action. I couldn't decide what to do.

The villagers settled the question while I was talk-ing to the umda. The night-watchman had gone out and the villagers had gathered—apparently they'd advanced on the dawar as a result of what he'd said to them. I heard something about wanting to taste the umda's blood, and about revenge, land, honour, the revoked land reform, and how the police had to be told what had happened. Someone went up to the umda and told him to act quickly, but before he could do anything I acted myself. I took my men and left the gun-room, passing through a sea of people. I was amazed at how many there were; I had no idea where this huge crowd had come from.

It was difficult to get to the vehicle, and pushing through the crowd I caught snatches of talk. The villagers were asking me to inform the district police station, and to move quickly before the umda's men had time to attack me. The case, they said, could be clearly proved; the evidence was there and, for the first time, the umda had left himself open to pros-ecution. If I abandoned the body, I'd be responsible. One man came up to me as I was trying to get into the vehicle and explained that they'd only just learned that the umda had sent the night-watchman's son to the army in place of his own son. Now it had to be brought out into the open, he said.

'How much longer are we going to put up with all this?' he asked. He seemed to have had a certain amount of education. 'Even in war!' he went on. 'We've sat back while they corrupted everything in Egypt: the land, the water, the air, the people. But the honour of defending Egypt's soil! Never!'

The man's words made me realize that this was an outright crime, and I felt as if my hands were stained with the blood of the body in the coffin. I had to act. This was a unique, ingenious kind of crime—not robbery or murder or even the forging of official papers. It was a crime no name had been invented for, since it had never been committed before, in Egypt or anywhere else. Immediate action was necessary, for who could guarantee it wouldn't happen again, as long as there were men like the umda in Egypt? And if it did happen again, who'd defend Egypt in the future?

The umda and his men came out, and I could see the guns and sticks; but the sea of people prevented them from getting to me. The deceased's friend arrived, together with the father. I don't know how we all managed to squeeze in next to the driver. The father's quiet weeping didn't stop till Masri's friend told him we were on his side and wouldn't abandon him, and that he'd get his rights—that was a promise from both of us, he said. At this the man calmed down, though I could still see two tracks of shining tears making their way through the mass of wrinkles and hollows in his old-man's face.

I shouted to the driver to get moving, and, like

magic, the sea of people opened up for the vehicle. Several of them jumped on the running-boards and the front end, hardly leaving the driver an opening to see the road. The crowd pushed at the vehicle with their chests, before the engine had started, to get it moving. Shots were fired, but I didn't know if they were meant to hit the vehicle or just frighten people. We set off for the district police station.

When we arrived, I found that the officer on duty was a young man my own age, with two stars on each shoulder; like me, he was from Cairo, though not from the same area. I briefly explained the situation, and asked him to open an investigation. I was exhausted, and all the excitement was visible in my face. He ordered me a glass of tea, and we talked as we waited. He wanted to familiarize himself with the case. Because it was so serious, he asked if he might consult the *ma'mur*,* who in turn ordered him to fetch the district prosecutor. When they'd all arrived, they got out their papers and pens.

I heard someone say, 'Question: What do you have to say about all this?' And I began my answer.

Ma'mur: the officer in charge of the district police station and administrative centre.

6
The Investigator

Midnight fascinates me. I look at it as the line dividing a day that's over and done with from one we know nothing about but the name. Twelve monotonous strokes from a nearby radio, the breath of approaching winter pervading the night; a night in the country during the closing days of Ramadan. Last night and the night before went by with no one witnessing Laylat al-Qadr. Only one more night left. After that, perhaps, the feast will come,* and people will have to put off their dreams till next year.

At midnight I get ready for bed. I never know when I'll manage to get to sleep, when I'll be delivered from this burning wakefulness, but at any rate sleep will come eventually.

Tonight they came from the district administration (there are knocks on the door every evening). It was an official summons involving a case they said was important, even grave. I wondered what case isn't supposed to be important and grave.

I asked the detective whether the duty officer in

---

* The Muslim feast of Ramadan, which celebrates the end of the month of fasting, is determined by the appearance of the new moon, not by a pre-established date.

the district administration had conducted the pre-liminary investigation into the case. No, he hadn't, he said; he'd conducted an oral inquiry, and then contacted the ma'mur, who, when he arrived, had sent him to notify me. He'd also informed the military counsellor at the *Muhafaza*, the provincial administration.

'Is it murder, theft, assault or a riot?' I asked the detective, while I got dressed.

Laughing, he replied that he didn't know quite what sort of case it was; all he knew for certain was that an army hearse had arrived at the district administration about an hour ago, bringing the body of a soldier who'd been killed in action. An officer had come with the vehicle, together with some soldiers from one of the villages in the district. I dressed quickly, and was soon out in the street. I live in a small district town in the Delta, where people go to bed at ten o'clock, though right now, since it's Ramadan, they stay up at night. I found the duty officer, the ma'mur and the intelligence officer in the district police station, and it was all systems go, as they say. I sat down with the duty officer and asked him to tell me what had happened.

The young police officer was so excited and upset that he talked at great length. Unlike the rest of us, he doesn't have his own chapter in this story, so I'll tell you everything he said just as I heard it from him, even the things that have no bearing on the case.

The young officer sat back in his chair and began: 'I was the officer on duty at the district police station, and I had nothing to do; there's usually nothing to do after the breaking of the fast during Ramadan. After the call to evening prayer I was standing at the window in the desk officer's room, with my nose pressed against the glass and the breath from my nostrils steaming up the window pane. I was drawing lines on the glass with my finger, when I noticed a black hearse coming slowly towards the station. When it came below the lamp post I could see its outlines clearly; then, moving out of the patch of light, it vanished into the dark night. The vehicle slowed down in front of the station and parked in the large, open square opposite. I noticed that the front plate was the colour of desert sand and the number of the vehicle was painted black, with the word 'army' underneath it. I realized then that this had something to do with the war.

'I left the desk room and went to stand at the station door. The door of the vehicle opened and a young officer stepped out, a very young first lieutenant. After him came a soldier in fatigues and an elderly peasant. Then the rear door opened, and two soldiers and a civilian got out, all looking as if they'd come a long way. At last I had some work to fill up the long, empty hours of the night. Despite the cold, I could see drops of sweat on the faces of the men.

'I welcomed the officer warmly and brought chairs for him and the people with him; then, when he'd settled down opposite me, I asked what I could do for him.

'He didn't say anything for a while, and when he did speak I knew I was up against a strange problem that had never arisen before. The umda involved is one of the most feared men in the district. Faced with this unique situation, I didn't know what to do; I just thanked God the ma'mur lived near the police station, directly opposite in fact, and that he was at home. I decided to consult him.

'I found the ma'mur playing chess with his eldest

son. The room was well heated against the cold of the October night. I got someone to announce me and apologized for intruding, then told him the story. At first he was quite upset, then he pulled himself together and authorized me to proceed with the necessary legal steps, promising to join me shortly. I had the deceased's belongings sealed, and sent word to you; the ma'mur was at the station by the time you arrived.'

I then began my investigation. The army officer was brought in and summarized the case: he'd come from Cairo to deliver the body of a soldier killed in action and had discovered that the man bearing the name of the deceased was alive and well, while the body he was transporting was that of someone else who'd gone into the army in his place. The officer was exhausted, his face was lined with fatigue and trickles of sweat. I had doubts as to the truth of his story, but at the same time I was struck by the remarkable assurance with which he spoke. I questioned him at great length. Then I looked over the names of the people who'd come with him.

I began with the dead man's friend. Sitting opposite me, he told me the whole story, while I wavered between astonishment and disbelief. I asked him if he had any personal papers that had belonged to the deceased before he changed from the watchman's son into the umda's son. Where was his former identity card, for example, or his student card?

He asked to see the deceased's belongings, and I gave them to him. He took out the army identity card and split it open. Hidden inside was a carefully folded piece of paper, which he took out and spread before me; it was a preparatory school certificate. The deceased's friend placed the certificate and the identity card side by side, and they were like the two

sides of a coin, reflecting the eternal contrast between the known and the unknown. The card we'd
all seen purported to be the identity card of the
umda's son, supposedly a soldier in the army; lying
next to it was a document showing that it was the
watchman's son who'd gone in to the army, in place
of the umda's son. In such an assignment, performance by proxy is never legally valid, whatever
authority sanctions it.

I had in my hands the first of the threads leading to
the truth. Entered on the certificate was the number
of Masri's identity card and its date of issue. I checked
it. The other card, found among his possessions, had
Masri's photograph together with the name of the
umda's son; but the two numbers and dates of issue
did not match, even though the same authority had
written them up: the Civil Registry Office in the
district administration. I was puzzled. Had he been
issued with more than one card? I confess that this
small point spurred me on to uncover the whole
truth. All my senses were alert, and my heart
thumped, sending the blood coursing through my
veins. I took off my jacket and hung it up. Up to now
I had been working half-heartedly, because the case
hadn't been clear in my mind.

Now I took out a piece of paper and listed the
people I would have to interview:

1. Masri's father, the former night-watchman, now
   pensioned off.
2. The village umda.
3. The umda's youngest son, whose name the deceased bears.
4. The recruiting officer in the district administration who was in charge of the office when the
   deceased was recruited.

On another sheet I wrote down the documents that would be required:

1. The forms kept at the Civil Registry Office in the district administration, on the basis of which the two identity cards were issued; also, the photographs on file.
2. Copies of the birth certificates of the deceased and the umda's son.
3. A statement setting out their status with respect to military service and all the papers and documents connected with their recruitment, whatever their relative importance.
4. A statement concerning the level of education attained by each of them; and, if either of them is studying now, what stage of education is involved.
5. The report of an extensive investigation into the case, with the aim of discovering the whole truth, carried out in person by the intelligence officer of the police station.

I launched into the investigation. After a little while the ma'mur of the district police station came to see me. He advised me to wait for the military counsellor from the Muhafaza. I asked him what the military counsellor had to do with it, and he said the case had a military dimension and probably a political one as well, so his opinion definitely had to be sought. I told him that this was an open-and-shut case; I'd go ahead with the investigation, and when the military counsellor arrived he would see whether there was anything for him to do. I resumed my work, but the ma'mur came to see me again, this time to remind me of the regulations about the body: I should either permit the burial to go ahead or authorize a pathologist to take whatever action was called for by the investigation. I then realized that I'd forgotten all about the body, which was actually the first matter to be attended to, and I sent for the officer who'd brought it.

I examined the documents concerning the death in action, taking my time and inspecting them minutely. I had good reason for this, since the case raised so many questions that I was beginning to doubt whether my hands had five fingers, whether each finger had a nail at the end, and whether the sky lay above the earth.

I made a cursory examination of the body and had some photographs taken of the face, then gave permission for burial. Photographs are important; they can settle a lot of questions in an investigation. But there was a problem. How could the body be buried when the whole village knew what had happened? How could we be sure there wouldn't be trouble?

I was surprised the ma'mur wanted to wait for the military counsellor and a representative from the Muhafaza and to get the opinion of the political authorities before the burial took place. He told me that he'd prefer the body to be taken to the district hospital rather than lying in the vehicle so long. I agreed, in the belief that I was honouring the body of a martyr who'd given his life to defend my country, my family and myself. Unfortunately, it later became clear that I'd made a mistake—but that's another story.

Next I had the witnesses brought in for questioning. I won't give you a summary of everything they said, because you've heard most of it already.

Some of the witnesses confessed spontaneously. What the real father of the deceased said, between his tears, was very moving, and we all felt sorry for him. The umda didn't confess, however, and I couldn't get a word out of him about his part in the affair. I had the watchman confront him and showed him the papers I had, reminding him that his land had been returned and that a part of this land was the plot that had belonged to the watchman. He replied that this had no bearing on the case. There were times when he was stuck for an answer, but he still refused to budge, and his eyes were empty of remorse. His voice was relaxed, laden with the smell of meat and fat and chicken and turkey. The flesh of his face and hands lay in folds.

I asked him about his son's military service, and he said that it had been deferred till he finished his studies. When I asked for evidence of this, he said he'd given the document to the school and couldn't get hold of it for the moment. Where had it been issued, I asked him. For the first time he was at a loss, but finally said he'd got it in Alexandria. I confronted him with the official military card confirming that his son was now an army recruit. He stammered out a few words, but didn't give a proper answer.

Questioning the umda was a laborious business; we kept going round in circles. Several times I cornered him, and brought him close to confessing, but still he wouldn't do it. I wondered what he was waiting for. Why didn't he confess and spare us both this distressing question-and-answer session? He was obviously waiting for some way out of this embarrassing predicament. I was quite upset about it all, but he seemed to regard it as commonplace.

One question kept bothering me during the investigation: who was the mastermind who'd cooked up the whole unusual affair, with all its ingenious ins-and-outs? He'd left a few loopholes, of course, but minor ones, which normally wouldn't have exposed the plan. I finally found out who he was: he was called 'the broker'. Several witnesses had referred to him in this way, and at first I thought 'Broker' must be his surname. Later they brought him in. He was like a man who'd abandoned all hope, and he didn't give me much trouble. He confessed to everything he'd done, but assured me several times, quite sincerely, that this was his last job and that he was going to turn over a new leaf. I would have liked to give you a full account of the broker's defence, but there isn't time, and I must be brief.

He was surprised, he told me, that the investigation was being carried out at all. 'A gallant, noble-hearted Egyptian', he said, 'decided to do someone else a favour. Don't you hear people in the street saying to each other, "I'll lay down my life for you"? Doesn't the state itself, through its official channels, call on us to give our lives for our fellow-citizens and our brothers in the faith? And if we don't volunteer, the state pays to buy our lives. That's exactly what happened here. The watchman's son decided to take on a patriotic assignment in place of the umda's son, and he must have done it willingly or he would have objected in some way. No one could have forced him to go against his will.

'There's another point I ought to raise too, because the umda refuses to bring it up. (He comes from a good family and doesn't like to blow his own horn.) The arrangement involved an exchange of mutual benefits—it was basically an economic transaction. Masri went to the army in place of the umda's son, and the watchman got two things in return. First of all, he got a steady job with a fixed wage, even though he's receiving a pension. As you know, the law strictly prohibits anyone from drawing a wage when he's on a pension—it's a criminal offence. In this case the umda, by doing the watchman a good turn, was covering up for a man who'd broken the law and laid himself open to prosecution under the Egyptian penal code; and don't forget that it's the umda who's responsible for making sure the law's enforced, so he got himself in even deeper.

'Second, the watchman got a plot of land measuring no less than five feddans. The just decisions recently adopted in Egypt make it quite clear that land seized by the Land Reform Agency should be restored to its owners. The umda got his land back and he has the right to use it for his own profit and so confirm the justice of the new measures and the injustice of the earlier seizure. Just imagine the umda's joy at getting his land back, after the long years he'd been forcibly and unjustly deprived of it! But the umda suppressed the joy he felt and, of his own free will, let the watchman keep the land—an action directly counter to the recent measures. The umda let him keep this land in exchange for the favour the watchman's son volunteered to do, even begged to do, without anyone asking him to.

'Besides, the watchman's son always wanted to join the army anyway. I swear he'd talked to me about it; in fact he'd actually volunteered to go, but they rejected him for some reason. This young man had high aspirations, and the aspirations of the poor usually destroy them. He was looking to the future, when some day he'd be an officer, his shoulders decorated with the eagle and stars, the crossed baton and sword. That's why he went, to achieve his personal ambition—he was the one who asked to go.

'Is it the umda's fault that he helped an Egyptian citizen to realize his aspirations? Note that he's an umda and also a father; in both his public capacity and as a private citizen, he's a shepherd for all these people and responsible for seeing that each of them fulfils his aspirations. The way he acted towards the watchman's son is in line with his duties as village umda.

'The last defence I'm going to make—and it will destroy the whole case—is that the umda's father was an umda, and so was his grandfather's grandfather. In other words, he comes from good stock. As for the watchman and his son, they belong to the class who go to bed hungry. The man's a labourer in the umda's fields. The umda owns the land and he owns whoever lives and works on it, so the watchman's son is the umda's property, to do with as he likes. They work on a farm that belongs to the umda, who has the right to use everything on that farm the way he sees fit.

'I object to this investigation on the grounds that it's an attempt to avoid facing the real issues. The problem you should be working on is this: now that the watchman's son has been killed in action while replacing the umda's son, which of the two is to be considered a martyr? We'll clearly have to consult the legal authorities, and read some history to find out if there's a precedent for this, and if there is, how it was dealt with; then we'll be able to decide the question of who's the martyr—the watchman's son who went in person, or the umda's son who had someone else die as a martyr in his place.

'Dependent on that decision is the solution to another problem that'll soon crop up: who is the deceased's beneficiary? Is it the umda or the watchman? As things stand, the person officially entitled to these benefits—and they are considerable—is the umda. But what about the poor watchman? Shall we trust to the umda's conscience, and ask him to give the money, wholly or in part, to the watchman? He's free to do that. Or should it be divided between them?

'What happened can't be considered a crime, because it was a lawful transaction. Aren't people allowed to vote by proxy in elections? An election is a patriotic activity, so if it's possible to appoint a representative there, it must be permissible in warfare too. The whole thing's over and done with anyway—it's no use crying over spilt milk. But what does need investigating is who will be the deceased's beneficiary. That's the important question.

'And again, why all this minute examination of everything? A man volunteered to give his life for another man—what's that got to do with the government? The days of red tape are over, so we're told, and we're living in an age of freedom. Every man's free to do as he likes with his life—he can shed his own blood if he wants to. In this case, one man gave his life's blood in another man's place. What's that got to do with the law? Just decide who will be the deceased's beneficiary, and may God guide you.'

I confronted him with the fact that actually the umda hadn't given the land to the watchman at all. In fact he'd exploited him by giving him three feddans under a temporary share-cropping contract—a system that happens to be against the law. He shouted that this wasn't true. The people who'd told me that, he said, were schemers intent on spreading lies.

I said I'd found out about it during my investigation, from the watchman himself, but he replied that the umda had enemies who'd turned against him after his land had been given back to him. They just wanted to distort things, he said.

I dismissed this extraordinary broker, who was mainly defending himself rather than the umda. But I was disturbed by what he'd said about the matter of the beneficiary. I realized that while my duty was to give a judgement about what had happened in the past, the most difficult job would be dealing with what would happen in the future. It might be important, at that moment, to ask, 'Who fought, died in action and won the victory?' But the more important question was: 'Who gained the moral victory . . . and the financial benefits?' That question was absolutely vital.

Now I had all the elements of the case before me. I had to gather the scattered ends in my mind and get things down on paper so I could sort it all out. I began by arranging the documents, starting with the two birth certificates. This was the only instance in which the details of the umda's son and the watchman's son agreed. They were both born on the same day and in the same village; that was indisputable. In all the other documents, their particulars pointed in completely different directions. As far as education was concerned, the watchman's son was an outstandingly successful pupil, but never completed his studies because his father couldn't meet the necessary expenses. The umda's son, on the other hand, had failed his examinations several times. The two applications for identity cards contained different information and different photographs: one face was clearly that of an umda's son, the other of a mere watchman's son. Their positions with respect to military service were also exactly opposite. The watchman's son was exempted from military service because he was an only son (he had sisters, but no brothers), while the umda's son had actually been called up for army service. His papers gave the date of his enlistment and showed that, after being given a numbered travel permit, he'd been transferred to the recruitment camp at Alexandria under the charge of a member of the army. The fingerprints on the papers were clearly those of two different people. The case was complete. Nothing remained except the umda's confession, and his position was extremely shaky after the evidence of the broker, who was reckoned to be his accomplice: the umda was the principal perpetrator, while the broker was his accessory.

I confronted the umda with all the facts, both old and new, but he wouldn't budge; he refused to confess. I then issued arrest warrants for the umda's son and the broker, hoping to exert some pressure on the umda, and get him to confess to what had happened. He was furious at his son's arrest, but still wouldn't confess. Again I sensed he was waiting for something, some new development that would give him a way out.

At this point I stopped work. I'd decided to take it easy for a bit. What I'd done so far had been extremely difficult, and I had to wait for the results of the investigations I'd ordered.

After a while the intelligence officer came to see me. I expected him to hand me a written report, which would then be either added to the file or given back to him if his findings were already known and therefore of no use in the investigation. To my surprise, he gave me an oral account—one that confirmed what had actually happened. The watchman's son, he said, had in fact been sent to the front in place of the umda's son, but he asked me not to bother taking the case any further, as it would eventually be dropped anyway.

There were two reasons for this, he said. First, he'd learned in the course of the inquiry that the umda was a man with a lot of influence; he had ready access, at any time and in any circumstance, to powerful people and top government officials. As soon as the investigation began and the case was formulated, he said, he'd been certain of one thing: the investigation would be dropped no matter what. This would come about in one of two ways: either on the strength of a request from the real father of the deceased, who'd say the case should be suspended in the interests of the precious memory of his son and out of respect for his sacred martyrdom; or instructions would come from higher up. He assured me that the second possibility reflected his own view of what would happen, but not anything he'd been told by anyone else—it was his personal opinion.

I asked him to set out the results of his inquiry in a brief official report, and to submit it to me through the ma'mur of the district police station. I would then proceed according to the factual evidence given in the report.

The umda was nowhere to be found and I was told he'd gone home to his village to rest, but was willing to come back at any time. He had several cars at his disposal and a telephone in his house, apart from the public state-owned telephone in his dawar, with a direct line to all the telephones of the district administration, the central police station and the provincial capital.

A large group of peasants from the village came to see me to complain about the umda's endless injustices. I made it clear to them that I was investigating a particular incident and couldn't look into anything else unless it had a direct bearing on the Masri case; to which they replied that this was merely one instance among thousands that showed how the umda treated them, the only difference being that this time he had been found out and we had heard about it. One young man among them said that all the umda's crimes were political. It was totally mistaken, he said, to deal with them by applying legal texts, because the loopholes in the texts—and there was no shortage of them—might well allow him to get off scot-free. The list of the umda's crimes is long, but it's not for me to go into them—and I'm sure the umda never referred to them in what he told you himself.

On reflection, it seemed to me that all these people should be regarded, indirectly, as witnesses for the prosecution; but they were afraid of the umda. I assured them their names would not be revealed; no one else would know who they were. I saw them as reserve witnesses who might be needed in my battle against the umda.

When the military counsellor from the Muhafaza arrived, along with a representative of the military police, I imagined they would co-operate with me in arriving at the truth. But what the man from the military police said shocked me. He criticized me for taking on a case that was a hundred per cent military without having the military police present, and without even notifying them, whereas in fact they alone were authorized to deal with it. The officers and soldiers who'd given me evidence would be called to account, he said, because military regulations clearly and unequivocally state that a hearing involving a member of the armed forces can be held only if an army representative is present. The law stipulates, he

168

added, that any other investigation must be carried out under their supervision.

I refused, on the grounds that the whole incident had occurred here, a long way from any army camp and from the army in general; the investigation therefore had to be carried to its conclusion no matter what.

Suddenly I received clear and unmistakable instructions to close the case, to forget all about it and bury the body. In fact it had been buried as soon as the instructions were issued, without my permission. The deceased was buried as the umda's son, not as Masri the watchman's son, even though this gave rise to two serious problems. First, it was ridiculous for him to be buried as the umda's son when another man bearing that name and answering to his description was alive and well. This meant that there were two people with the same name, one dead and the other still alive, so that in future it would be difficult to decide which was the original and which the replacement. The other problem was Masri—where was he supposed to be? Actually this problem didn't emerge just with his burial. It had been implicit for some time, for ever since Masri had gone away as the umda's son he'd faced the problem of establishing his own existence. On top of all that was the realization that Masri—who'd left home, joined the army, fought and died in action—was deprived even of being remembered as a martyr.

I tried to point all this out, but the military counsellor from the Muhafaza refused to listen. The country was going through critical times, he said. Wasn't this the first time in the whole of history, ancient, medieval and modern, that the Arabs had triumphed? The Masri episode might cast gloomy shadows over the victory that Egypt and the Arabs had been awaiting for thousands of years. He implored me to consider what Egypt's enemies would say if they heard about the case.

'Moreover,' he went on, 'the whole incident isn't important enough to warrant all this attention. As the nation and society advance and develop, the process crushes thousands of individuals in the interest of the community as a whole. It's enough for Masri that he's given his life in battle for his country. It's not important what name he gave it under; what matters is that he shed his blood as a sacrifice for his country, his family and the Egyptian people. Whether he shed it as Masri or the umda's son, is secondary.

'Don't forget that at that moment all of Egypt was summed up in a single sentence: "When the whole becomes one, the whole exists in one." Do you undertand what it means to talk of individual features melting into one? How I wish the present generation could grasp the meaning of patriotism! How I wish they could understand the meaning of the whole existing in one!'

I objected to his closing the case. For the life of me I couldn't understand how he could pretend it all had never happened. I'm an investigator and my job is to find out the truth. I have moments of satisfaction in my work, and moments of anger too, but this is my personal affair. This case was special, an investigator had to break his back pursuing it—I would get close to the truth only to find it playing hide-and-seek with me. It was like running through a maze. Getting at the truth is what gives me pleasure—failure causes me acute distress, it lies on me like lead. Why am I twisting and turning like this as I come to the most serious part of the story? Well, let me say what I

170

have to say.

I was absorbed in the details of the case—questions, answers, papers, reports—when someone in high authority sent for me. I was delighted at this, thinking that 'they' had heard of the case—that at last it had come to the ears of the people who had the final say. This was proof of its significance, I thought, and also a guarantee that the person who'd been wronged would be given his rights and the wrong-doer punished.

I went to see this important person. Once we were inside the limousine they'd sent for me, the chauffeur pressed a button and the windows shot up. There was a milk-white telephone in front of me, and the air inside the car was unlike anything I'd breathed before. I asked the driver for the secret of this fragrant air, but he couldn't be bothered to answer and just pointed at a small, complicated-looking gadget on the dashboard. I repeated my question. 'Air conditioning,' he said brusquely, and that was all the explanation I got.

So the vehicle was air-conditioned. Sitting in this relaxing atmosphere, I began to think over my part in the case. I was happy. We really were living in a golden age, I thought—here were people in top positions taking an interest in a case like this. That's the most important thing a ruler can do, to make sure that justice reaches down to the lowest of the people. It's been said that authority is founded on justice, that the just ruler is the one who never rests as long as a single one of his subjects is hungry or naked or without shelter; the man who said that knew the difference between righteous rulers and the other sort! Reflecting on all this, I said to myself, 'May this case I'm now investigating shake the mountains to their very foundations!' We were dealing with blood shed in defence of the country, and the smell of blood mingled with desert sand was still in the air.

When I arrived at the top man's place, it seemed to me that the car was just a mobile extension of his office, or perhaps his office was the stationary extension of the car. The air was fragrant and warm, the myriad colours seemed as unreal as a rainbow. His greeting was lukewarm; I didn't know if that was his usual way of welcoming people or if he'd put it on for me.

I didn't say anything; I was waiting for him to question me, so I could tell him I was nearing the end of my investigation, with only the umda's confession needed to complete the case. I'd also tell him that this confession wasn't really crucial, since the evidence of the witnesses all pointed in the same direction. The broker's defence was an example. He was the umda's accessory from start to finish, and his defence was virtually a full confession, made by a person who, from a legal standpoint, was a prime accomplice. I decided that when the top man gave me the chance to speak, I'd ask for a swift and decisive trial, for a verdict within ten days at the most, because of the case's bearing on national defence.

The top man got up from his chair and moved out from behind his magnificent desk. He walked to one of the windows, drew back the curtain, and turned his back on me to look down into a small square below. With the first warning signs of winter, people were suddenly faced with a cold they weren't yet used to. The top man smiled, his smile broadened into a laugh, and then he suddenly grew serious as he turned to me and asked, 'When will you be through with this business you're working on?'

I sat up straight, took a breath and swallowed, but before I could answer, he said, 'Don't make a speech, just answer my question. First, have you finished the investigation?'

'There's still one last part,' I said, trying to ease the situation, 'the confession of the accused, the original perpetrator of the crime, but I'll get it today, or tomorrow at the latest.'

'Is there any reason why he shouldn't make a confession today?'

'He refuses to confess, in spite of the evidence of prosecution witnesses.'

'In that case how much is his evidence worth?'

'In the speedy trial that I'm urging, the lack of a confession will be considered a flaw in the procedure, and the judge may accordingly call for a new investigation; or he may investigate the case himself, which would delay the whole thing.'

'Did you say trial?' asked the top man in amazement.

'Of course,' I replied naively. 'After the prosecutor's investigation, the case is supposed to go to court.'

'What case?'

'The case I'm investigating, about the man killed in action.'

'What man killed in action?'

'Masri, the watchman's son.'

'What watchman's son?'

'The one who went into the army in place of the umda's son.'

'What umda?'

'The umda of the village. He's said to have a lot of powerful connections, but his crime's quite clear.'

'What do you mean, "clear"?'

'I mean that the basic elements of the crime are

quite clear: the criminals, the witnesses, the material evidence, the victim . . .'

'What victim?'

'Victims, I should have said.'

'What are you talking about, man?' His voice was louder this time.

I decided not to answer. This was getting ridiculous, and I wonder what he was getting at. Had he really sent for me, or had he meant to summon someone else? A sudden sense of impotence crept over me; I seemed to be in a very difficult position. I thought of shouting, screaming, running, pouncing on him, but many things held me back: the size of the office, the security measures I'd passed through before finally being given the honour of meeting him, the guard posts and check-points, the car that had brought me, his anonymity . . . On my way to see him I'd asked who it was I was going to meet. The answer had been brief: 'Someone in a very high position.'

'Who is he?' I'd asked. 'Which government department is he responsible for?' The answer was the same: 'Just someone in a very high position.'

'Listen,' he now said, jabbing his finger at me.

'There's no case, no nothing. The peasants in the village hatched the whole thing by making up a criminal case like something from a detective novel. The watchman's son joined the army and, well aware of his low origins, wanted to be associated with distinguished, high-born people. He wrote out false statements from the very first day, linking himself to the umda (whose office is hereditary) by saying that he was his son. So when he was killed in action, he died as a martyr under a name he'd assumed of his own free will, and that's all there is to it!

Consequently, his martyrdom will be recorded under that name, and he has been buried as the umda's son.

'There's no case, understand? A young man became a martyr. Fine! His place in paradise is assured. And if he made a mistake before his martyrdom, if his ambition drove him to take the name of a distinguished family, that's not our problem!

'Quite apart from all that, who ordered you to carry out this investigation anyway? I know what you're going to say—a citizen reported something to the police, the police did a preliminary investigation and the case was then turned over to the district prosecutor's office. That's all quite proper as far as procedure goes, but you've made several important mistakes.

'First, you were aware from the outset that it wasn't a civilian case. The military discussion is about ninety per cent of it; in fact, it would be more true to say that it's a military case pure and simple. And the army has a system of jurisdiction of its own—its own police, investigators, courts. Don't you realize the army even has its own laws, which are different from those of the civil courts? Yet in spite of all this, you launched straight into the investigation, without making any attempt to contact the relevant military authorities. They aren't so far away, you know, and they would have taken over the whole case.

'Second, I assume you plunged into this investigation out of patriotic zeal and conscientious professionalism. You imagined, and you persist even now in imagining, that you were dealing with a crime, and so you felt obliged to investigate it. There's nothing wrong with that—but should every

175

investigation be public, with all the parties concerned knowing all about it? I don't think so; in fact I totally disagree. Some cases have to be dealt with in secret, and this case is a prime example. The war in which Masri lost his life is still going on right now, while we're sitting here talking. True, we've accepted a cease-fire, but only for a limited period. Eventually we have to liberate all our occupied land, which means we're still in a state of war with our national enemies. The whole country's in a state of emergency. The investigation should have been kept secret.

'You know that every Egyptian family has a son in this war of liberation. I ask you, in all sincerity, to imagine how these families would feel if, with the war still going on, they saw the body of someone killed in action being dragged round the country with no one willing to bury it, on the pretext of an investigation into the identity of the dead man and his beneficiary. The secrecy of this investigation is a patriotic issue, no less so than the war itself. Who can be sure that this war will be the last? Can you? Can anyone? We'll certainly be fighting again soon — and probably in the distant future as well.

'If a new war does start, your investigation will do a lot of damage. Can you imagine the impression the case would make if people heard about it, the public opinion at home and abroad? It would cast a shadow over our war, our victory, our heroes, and who would benefit from that? The watchman and his son? Every Egyptian was called upon to make some sacrifice, and the watchman sacrificed his son, for which he deserves our thanks.

'We've considered the matter at length, and there was a strong body of opinion that you should be disciplined for these disastrous mistakes, but I

176

opposed that, for the simple reason that I'm sure you meant well, and that none of these mistakes was the result of any deliberate ill will. My decision is this: you're to forget all about the investigation. Close the official report and bring all the investigation papers to me. I've instructed all parties concerned to take the necessary steps.'

He raised his hand in a theatrical gesture of dismissal and shouted, 'That will be all!'

Hidden hands opened the door from the outside, and the top man pointed to make it clear he wanted me to leave. Trembling with emotion, I went straight back to my office, where I found that strict orders had arrived long before, issued by this top man whose name, position and identity were a complete mystery to me. Apparently the messenger who'd come to summon me had also brought the final instructions.

I found out that the ma'mur had dismissed criminals, victims and witnesses alike, and had let the umda's son go free. All I had now were the papers and documents of the investigation, which I'd locked away. I gathered them up and decided to put them where I wouldn't lose them, till I could meet my superiors and put the matter to them.

My own position was that the investigation should be carried to its natural conclusion no matter what; this is how it must be, I felt, in view of the clearly established case I had before me. The problem was with the word 'must'. Whoever may have the right to use it in everyday speech, I certainly don't. I haven't applied to join the 'Must' party in Egypt, and evidently I don't meet the membership conditions. Before I left my office—putting off the interview with my superiors till the next day—I put the papers relating to the case in my briefcase. I was determined to take them with me wherever I went.

Suddenly the deceased's real father, the watchman, burst in on me. He was a different man, utterly transformed in the short time since I'd last seen him. He knew well enough, he said, that we couldn't do anything to the umda. I replied that this wasn't so, that justice would run its course; no one in the country was above the law any more. Then I laughed at myself as I realized that he hadn't the faintest idea what I was talking about. I asked him, casually, who'd told him we couldn't do anything against the umda, and he said that it wasn't any one person; everyone had assured him of it. That's why he'd come to see me, against the instructions of his honour the ma'mur, who'd ordered him not to leave the village for any reason and on no account to go to the district administration.

The watchman had just two requests. First, in his capacity as the real father of the deceased, he was asking for the body to be handed over to him, so he could bury it; then he'd know where the body was and be able to perform the necessary rites in the future. Second, he wanted the money due the deceased's beneficiary. That was all he was asking; he'd be satisfied with that.

I was convinced of the justice of the man's requests, and I should have given instructions accordingly, but I thought it advisable to get the agreement of the ma'mur and the rest of those responsible. So I went to see the ma'mur, but he looked angry at the mere mention of the subject; he wasn't at all pleased about my concern with a case that was now closed. He listened to what I had to say with growing impatience.

'I thought', he said finally, 'that we'd finished with this strange business, which as far as I'm concerned has soured the taste of our country's victory. As for the body, it's true that according to civil and Islamic law it should be handed over to the deceased's family, but this is such a peculiar situation that it's not necessary to carry out the letter of the law.

'Who are we going to give the body to? If we give it to the umda, the watchman will protest—he's got proof that the deceased was his son. And he won't be alone; the whole village might rise up with him, and then it might not be easy to keep things under control.

'On the other hand, if we give the deceased's body to the watchman, measures will have to be taken against the umda and his son; and that would reopen a case which, according to clear and unambiguous instructions, is to be closed and forgotten.

'In view of all this, for the moment the safest course is not to give the body to either party—at least until things have settled down and people have had time to forget the whole business. Then we'll hand the body over to whoever can prove proper ownership. Until then the body's in our custody. We've buried it in a safe place, and it's well guarded. I assure you that moving the body now would bring nothing but trouble, and could be dangerous. Besides, I couldn't go to the village with the body—God only knows what might happen if I did. As for the second request, I'll get in touch with the authorities and find out what action to take.'

He picked up the government telephone next to him and, whispering so I couldn't hear, asked to be put in touch with the secretary of some person in authority. He got through quickly, and began by apologizing and promising that this would be the last inquiry about the case.

'What case?' asked the voice at the other end.

'This business of the false claim made by the watchman,' he answered. 'The claim that his son went to war in place of the umda's son and was killed in action.'

I opened my mouth to set the matter straight, but he motioned to me to be quiet. He didn't speak for some moments, just listened to a great deal of talk from the other end; then he again promised that this question would be the last.

He hung up and wiped sweat from his brow. 'I've consulted the highest authorities,' he said, 'and they were astonished that the question should even be asked. They were also astonished that we were still thinking about it, since we were supposed to have forgotten the whole investigation. According to government documents, the deceased's father was the umda, which makes him the beneficiary.

'The watchman won't get a millim unless the umda agrees; when the money is paid to the umda, he can give it to the watchman if he wants. Or he can sign a power of attorney making the watchman the official payee in his place.'

I tried to argue, but he answered that these were the instructions from the authorities and couldn't be disputed. We contacted the umda and asked him about the compensation money—would he renounce some of it in the watchman's favour? To my astonishment, he refused. It was a trifling sum, he said, no more than a few millims compared with his great wealth, but he wouldn't part with any of it because he wasn't going to fall into the trap we were laying for him. If he renounced it, that would suggest that he really had committed some crime; it would be tantamount to a confession that could be used against him. He assured us that once he received the money he might give the watchman some alms, but he wouldn't donate to him alone. He'd give to all the poor and needy, but from his own money, not from the money of the deceased; and as far as he was concerned, that was the end of it.

I asked the ma'mur if I could leave, to go and tell the watchman about this, but he asked me to stay. Then he summoned the watchman, who saluted him and treated him as if he was the most important man in the world. The ma'mur told him bluntly what he'd decided. There would be a delay in handing over the body, which for the moment would remain in the custody of the ma'mur himself. As for the money, we had agreed with the umda that he would let his conscience be his guide. The umda would never let him go empty-handed; all the watchman had to do was to go and see him. The umda was the descendant of a good family with a long history, and would never treat him unjustly.

The former watchman raised his hand in salute, clicked his heels and said with exaggerated deference, 'The orders of the ma'mur Bey will be obeyed.'

The watchman backed out of the spacious office. As he retreated he bumped into a screen and almost knocked it over, but he spun and grabbed it before it fell, then went out.

When I got back to my office I found him waiting for me outside the door. He made me swear his son's body was in safe keeping. I set his mind at rest, assuring him it would be handed over to him when things had died down. I told him this even though I hadn't the faintest idea where it was buried—it could have been in any one of Egypt's many cemeteries. He said he was afraid the umda wouldn't give him a single millim, and as I stood behind my desk I heard an alien voice coming from my throat, the voice of past days that will never return till the suffering in my heart abates. I told him, slowly, that the umda would give him everything he himself received, and that if he didn't he'd have me to deal with. I said I had the power to force the umda to give him the money.

The man called down blessings upon me, blessings that were heartfelt and sincere. I was pleased that I'd made him happy, though I had no faith whatever in my ability to keep my promise. He saluted and left, wearing his reassurance like a coat of paint on a dilapidated house.

As I sat there, I asked myself if I wasn't a party to the whole thing, if I couldn't be considered the main perpetrator. I should have given my instructions independent of anyone else, and the case should have been kept separate from everything that's happening in our country now. I came back to the word 'must', forgetting that I have no authority to use it. Even if I'd given my instructions, would they have been followed? I doubt it—but just to give them would have brought me a bit of comfort and self-respect in the days to come.

On my way home I felt calm. At least I had the papers, documents and legal evidence. And I mean to keep them; I'll never give them up no matter what happens. My quiet walk and the silence of late evening reminded me of the sense of peace I always felt on nights when I finished a case. I'd whisper, in the deserted streets, the words my mother used to say when I was a child long ago: 'That's the end of the story.'

I tried repeating it to myself: 'That's the end of the story.' I stopped and said it again. Then I asked myself, 'But is it really the end of the story?'

I'd asked a question, and it deserves a satisfactory answer, comprehensive, final and convincing. Since right now I don't know the answer, I'll have to start looking for it. If I fail, I'll drive the question from my heart, and let it wander the length and breadth of the land of Egypt, searching for its own answer. And when the question sets out on its journey, I'll follow it with another question: 'Will it ever find the answer?'

Afterword

The noted Egyptian intellectual Louis Awad has said that there are two outstanding writers in Egypt today, Gamal al-Ghaitani and Yusuf al-Qa'id. There are, indeed, literary voices that stand out among their peers, and one such voice is that of Qa'id.

Muhammad Yusuf al-Qa'id was born on 2 April 1944 in the village of al-Dahriyya in the coastal district of al-Buhaira, in what Egyptians refer to as the *rif*, a term that means 'countryside' but also has the connotation 'backwater'. Yusuf's father was one of that class of poor peasants who do not own even the tiny plots they work, and who have made up the silent majority of Egyptians ever since Pharaonic times. Among Egypt's intellectual elite (indeed, among any branch of that country's professionals), such an origin is unusual. Nasser himself was the grandson of peasants, but his father was a civil servant. Moreover, unlike many of Egypt's noted writers and intellectuals, Qa'id received all his education in his native land. He taught there for three years and served in the armed forces, witnessing the wars of 1967 and 1973. He is now the literary editor of the magazine *al-Musawwar*.

Qa'id is a prolific author, with eleven novels and

four short-story collections to his credit. His first novel appeared in 1969, and since then the novel has been his principal literary vehicle.

The Arabic novel is a relatively recent development, having arisen in the early years of the twentieth century. After an initial period of experimentation during which writers like al-Muwailihi and Hafiz Ibrahim sought to modernize traditional Arabic narrative forms, most prose writers in the Arab world opted for essentially Western forms of the novel and short story. The social and/or political novel has long held the greatest attraction for writers, and their novels have tended to be fairly classical, indeed conventional, in organization and narrative technique. In Egypt, they have also usually been set in the cities. When rural characters appear, it is generally after their arrival in Cairo or Alexandria.

With the advent of a new generation of Egyptian writers, however, much has changed in the Arab novel. There has been more emphasis on rural settings, on the *rif*. More important, however, is that although most new novels are still social, there have been radical shifts in their construction and organization.

Yusuf Qa'id is one of the most important representatives of this new generation. His novels combine a strong social conscience with an innovative use of narrative techniques. His trilogy, *The Complaints of the Eloquent Egyptian* (1981–1985), for instance, involves an author writing a novel, drafts of which are incorporated into the text, along with other documents. Another of his novels, *It Is Happening in Egypt Now* (1977), begins by inviting the reader to create the novel along with the author, and then goes on to provide a set of documents for that purpose.

War in the Land of Egypt grew out of a short story of the same title. The novel was written in 1975 but not published until 1978, and even then not in Egypt, but in Beirut. Its first Egyptian edition appeared only in 1985. (Although banned in its country of origin, however, *War in the Land of Egypt* was translated into Russian and Ukrainian.)

As in many of his other works, so in *War in the Land of Egypt* Qa'id introduces literary innovation primarily in the narrative itself, as the story is told by several characters, each of whom tells part of the tale. The technique of multiple narrators has been used before in Arab literature, most notably by the Egyptian author Naguib Mahfouz in his novel *Miramar* (1967). But Qa'id's use of the technique differs from Mahfouz's. Qa'id's characters do not each present the entirety of the plot; in fact, there is eventually no overlap in their narrations, and therefore little or no repetition of events. This permits the plot to unfold as it would in a standard narrative devoid of multiple voices, a distinctive exploitation of the technique that creates a narrative tension between the multiplicity of story-tellers and the continuous progression of the plot. The absence of repetition enhances the story's dramatic impact, while the variety of perspectives implicit in multiple narration is not sacrificed to clarity or drama. *War in the Land of Egypt* provides a microcosmic catalogue of Egyptian social types. It is almost as if a series of actors stepped forward, each to deliver his own monologue.

The technique of multiple narrators also evokes an issue central to much of Qa'id's fiction, that of artistic creation itself. The narrators express awareness of their own narrative roles. One character introduces himself by explaining that in this novel there is no author to do it for him. But the speakers are conscious of their co-narrators as well. The broker, for example, expresses his gratitude to the umda for having 'already told you' about something unpleasant. Similarly, when the investigator tells us that he will not specify the umda's long list of crimes, he adds that he is sure that the umda will not have mentioned this list in his own part of the story. At the same time, the interrelationship of the narrators shows that the technique is not merely a formal device but also a means of expressing conflict among the characters, a conflict which in turn reflects the contradictions of the Egyptian countryside.

None of the six narrators has a name, and together they represent all the major characters in the story save one, Masri, who has no narrative role. The first three narrators are directly involved in the life of the village, whereas the last three are external to rural life. The order in which the narrators take the floor is also significant. The first three show a progression from the character furthest from Masri towards the closest, his father. The order is the opposite for the last three narrators, Masri's army friend being the one closest to him, and the investigator standing completely outside the action. There is a movement towards and then away from a centre, which is Masri himself.

Masri's role, however, is ambiguous in several respects. He is the central character, yet he is the only one with no narrative voice; he has no chapter of his own to recount his version of events. Masri's voicelessness is related to his lack of power. All the other characters influence his destiny, and we watch as each in turn shapes his life. In this Masri is like many of Qa'id's other heroes, also marked by a basic lack of control over their lives.

But there is another sense in which Masri is distinct from the other characters: he is the only one with a name. But in a way his ownership of a name is only apparent. 'Masri' means 'Egyptian' and as such loses its specificity. That is why the friend, when he utters Masri's real name by mistake, is able to tell the officer that he was not using 'Masri' literally, that the name belongs to everyone in the country.

A name, of course, is part of a person's identity, and the ambiguity in Masri's name does more than simply allow him to stand for all Egyptians. It also reflects the confusion of identity central to the intrigue, for Masri's name and identity are as critical to the novel's organization as they are to its plot. He alone has a name, and yet that name is continually shrouded. When the friend asks Masri his name for the register, we expect him to answer, and indeed wonder what name he will give. But the author denies us the information. Masri may be the centre of the story, but he is an absent centre, absent as a narrator and in one sense absent as a character too, since his identity has been subsumed into that of the umda's son. Even his name which seems a presence compared with the designations of the other characters is a kind of absence, since a name that can refer to all Egyptians cannot really define any one of them. In that sense, the 'Egyptian' is denied more than mere justice: his very identity is threatened.

Other ideas are structured around this pivotal absence. One is a parallel between sons and land. The umda's offer, of course, is based on such a notion, but the connection goes deeper. Land and sons are both related to fecundity: the umda will trade his land for his son because he cannot create another son—he is impotent. At the same time, the trade is improper even psychologically, since the land is symbolically female and the son male. Normally they should complement and not replace each other.

But Qa'id's most consistent concern is the gap between rich and poor, the radical differences in their ways of life. The parallel between the two families—the umda's and the watchman's, with the two sons born on the same day—makes the contrast in social circumstances all the more glaring. Even their blood is different, according to the watchman: the umda's is blue, 'not like the grubby red blood of people like us'.

These inequalities are apparent to other characters too. According to the friend, the umda 'never tires of repeating that his power comes from God—which is apparently true! The simple truth is that if God has chosen to be Lord of the rich alone, then the poor's only recourse is to look for a Lord of their own.' This relationship between the poor and religion comes out again when the umda's clerk asks the watchman if he has seen Laylat al-Qadr and the watchman replies that it never occurred to him that this night had anything to with poor people. And when the officer hears the friend speak of 'Masri', he asks whether this is a nickname, to which the friend replies: 'Do the poor have nicknames?' The poor and the rich live different lives. There are two kinds of people, the night-watchman explains: 'the ones who get as much sleep as they want and the ones who don't.'

When the night-watchman is served dinner in the umda's house he is so awed by the meal that he can hardly eat. The meat he comments on the moment the tray is brought in is the very item he leaves, because he feels uncomfortable with the utensils. In the repeated references to food, meat, and eating— as in the investigator's description of the umda's voice as 'laden with the smell of meat and fat and chicken and turkey' or the watchman's recollection of the last time he had eaten meat as he kisses the umda's hand—food and the rich become almost consubstantial.

Qa'id's sociology, however, goes beyond the division between rich and poor. Intersecting this dichotomy is another: between city and country. People in the city live differently. The friend, for example, explains that staying up at night until the pre-dawn meal during the month of Ramadan is a custom of cityfolk like himself. When in the countryside, city dwellers like the friend and the officer feel like they're in a foreign country. A peasant tells the officer that he is obviously from the city, 'which swam in a sea of coloured lights from sunset to sunrise and was full of policemen armed to the teeth'. The friend finds the night 'filled with all the mysterious sounds of the country'. To him, it 'seemed like a secret code'.

In another passage the same character sees the countryside as filled with 'mystery and myth'. The Arabic word translated as 'myth' is *hikayat*, which literally means 'stories', a term also applied to tales told orally. In classical times, however, it referred as well to certain kinds of narrative literary texts, some of which were as long as novels. In a sense, the friend's phrase sums up both Qa'id's novelistic enterprise and his life. The mystery lies both in the country and at the center of his text. *War in the Land of Egypt*, too, is both of and from the countryside.

In this it is like its author.

Fedwa Malti-Douglas
Associate Professor, Oriental and
African Languages and Literature
University of Texas, Austin